MW01436114

The Ink Ghosts

Bex Archer

All characters, events and places in this publication are fictitious and any resemblance to real persons, living or dead, is purely coincidental.

Chapter 1

November 1907

I was eighteen years old the first time I set eyes on Creakie Hall. Dour and forbidding it stood on a rise in the land staring out across mile after empty mile of marsh and as soon as I saw it my enthusiasm for a fresh start died. Arnold, my brother, librarian, had promised it would be a step up, better wages for both of us. But as I looked at that dreary pile of bricks all thoughts of an improvement in our circumstances went clean out of my head. "It looks horrible, Arnold, can't we go back to Norwich?"

"No, you know we can't. The family don't need me anymore," he put our bags down onto the frozen driveway to rest his arms. The promised horse and trap hadn't met us at the railway station so we'd had to walk the two miles to Creakie Hall. I'd offered to carry the bags for a while, I was three inches taller and stronger, but his manly pride had been wounded by the suggestion and I wasn't going to offer only to be snapped at again.

"I could've stayed on by myself."

"So you keep saying. Anyway, it's too

late — we're here now so we must make the best of it."

But making the best of Creakie Hall was no easy task. We stood at the gateway between fancy, wrought iron gates that had long been left open and were being steadily smothered by the brambles and bindweed that held them fast. Dense, dark woodland backed the house on three sides. I was more used to being surrounded by houses than trees and the sight of it sent shivers down my spine. It was late afternoon, the time of day when any sensible person wants to go indoors to stoke up the fire and feel snug and cosy, to shut out the dark autumn nights with their slugs and snails, but Creakie Hall didn't look like the kind of house that understood cosy or snug. No homely, welcoming lights shone out to greet us. No one waved. No one shouted a cheery, 'Hello'. Arnold picked up our bags again and we trudged along the gloomy driveway. The ground was rock hard, all the mud frozen solid. Cracked, white ice covered the puddles laying in the deep ruts worn away by the wheels of carriages and carts. A sudden honking and cronking from overhead made me look up. From somewhere beyond the woodland a long skein of geese flew over the house heading towards the marsh, gliding down, disappearing into the green scrub. Dead leaves rustled and skittered under the knotty, old trees lining either side of the track, their bare, black twigs stretching out across the leaden sky like weeds caught in the flow of a strong river. "Those trees all bend the same way."

"Wind blasted," Arnold huffed and puffed. His white face was pinched, trousers flapping around his scrawny legs.

The cold bit through the soles of my best boots, "You should've worn your thick trousers. You must be frozen in those ones."

"These look smarter. We must make a good first impression. New start and all that. No more 'assistant librarian' — it's Mr Bunting, librarian, from now on."

I had been pleased for him, all his hard work had paid off, but I was a city girl and already missing our old place, its warmth and life. I moved my bag from my right hand to my left and wriggled my fingers, trying to get the blood moving in them again as we tramped on. The driveway curved around to the left separating the front of the house from the frost covered lawn. Either side of the front door long flowerbeds clung to the remains of the summer's blooms. Tangles of dead, brown stems were untended, uncared for, some broken down by the wind, some falling onto the driveway, all gone to seed. No gardener worth his salt would leave it looking so tatty so clearly there was no gardener or at least none that was good at his job.

"I should be round the back. Servants don't go in at the front door."

Arnold dumped our bags down onto the stone doorstep, "The letter was quite explicit, 'be sure to call at the front door'."

Caught by the wind dead leaves swirled around our feet. The step hadn't been swept in days, maybe weeks, "You said they've got money."

The door knocker, a great lion's head biting the grubby, brass ring in its mouth, squeaked as Arnold lifted it, "They have. Lots of it."

"Well if they've got so much how come it all looks so grubby?"

Arnold shrugged, "Can't get the staff. That's what you're here for." He banged the knocker against the brass striker and I could have sworn I heard an echo, the place felt so deserted, so hollow.

We waited … and waited. I jigged about, keeping moving, trying to stay warm. "There's nobody here. It's empty."

A hint of uncertainty crept into

Arnold's voice, "Of course there is. They just haven't heard us." He raised the knocker and hammered again, louder and longer.

I was frozen, longing to walk away, "This is horrible. It's creepy. I'm sure there's nobody here. We could go back to Norwich. If we hurry we could get the last train back. I don't know why we had to leave."

"You do know why so stop being daft. We're here to stay … and besides, I can't carry these bags all the way back again." He rubbed his hands together, "You'll soon make friends. Bound to be some young people around here."

I couldn't believe what I was hearing, "People? What people? Arnold, there's nothing here. Only a couple of houses and they were way back. We're in the middle of nowhere."

A dog barked inside. Arnold's shoulders slumped with relief, "See. Someone's in. I told you we were expected."

A woman's voice called, "Quiet, Tibbs, quiet. Silly boy. You'll scare them off." There was the steady tap of sensible heels walking over a hard floor, the handle turned and the front door creaked open, "Mr and Miss Bunting?" A short woman, middle-aged with salt-and-pepper hair, half gone grey, half still dark, didn't wait for us to answer but held out her hand, "Welcome to Creakie Hall."

Arnold shook her hand politely, "Thank you, Mrs…?"

"Miss," she corrected him, "Miss Lamb." She pulled the door wide open, "Do come in. The family are expecting you." Arnold picked up our bags and we stepped inside to be greeted by more barking. Tibbs, a big spaniel, brown, white and mostly dirty, whacked his tail against Miss Lamb's skirt leaving dirty marks on it. So many of his muddy paw prints covered the floor they almost hid the pattern of cream and black tiles and I thought, 'I suppose it'll be my job to clean that lot up.' Somewhere a man and woman were arguing, their voices raised behind a closed door.

"Thank you for coming to the front door. When I'm working in this part of the house I can't hear anyone knock on the back door. I should introduce myself properly. Miss Lamb. Housekeeper." She closed the front door behind us and adjusted the shawl around the shoulders of her neat, pin tucked blouse, "I believe that would be the most accurate term although currently there isn't much house to keep. Just the family, myself, and a woman from the village who comes in three times a week."

All my dreams of a house even livelier than the last one went up in smoke. The thought of being stuck there with only a housekeeper and a woman from the village for company was so disappointing it must've shown on my face, everything usually did.

I knew Miss Lamb had noticed because her forehead furrowed, "I do hope it won't be too quiet here for you."

"Not at all. Not at all," Arnold jumped in before I could answer. "We've been used to a city house, bit too noisy really. But Zilla's been looking forward to coming here — haven't you, Zilla!" He nudged his elbow discreetly into my ribs and I managed a half-hearted nod.

Miss Lamb's face lightened, "I'm sure you'll soon get used to it. There will be plenty of work to keep you busy … and there are quite a few young people in the village. You'll get to meet them all soon enough." She paused, the corners of her mouth lifting in a smile, "Zilla … that's an unusual name."

My mouth flapped like a dying fish and words gushed out, "Our Mum always said it was her little fancy. A for Arnold and Z for Zilla — A to Z, her first and last children — but it's just us — there were never any others in the middle."

I knew I'd said too much from the look on Arnold's face, "I'm sure Miss Lamb doesn't need to hear our family history."

Bless Miss Lamb, before my face had time to blush she said cheerily, "Not at all. There's no better start to knowing someone than learning about their name. Names should always come first, they can tell you so much about a person." She tweaked her shawl again, "Now, if you'd like to leave your bags and follow me I'll introduce you to the family. They're in the drawing room." As she set off across the hall I took a quick look around. No warmer inside than it was outside the still air clung onto the smell of stale tobacco and boiling cabbage with the occasional waft of wet dog. Pictures in wide gilt frames, mahogany chairs with padded seats of deep red damask, a weighty sideboard supporting tall, fancy, chinese vases and a stuffed owl under a glass dome, all had lost their shine, all covered in a heavy layer of dust. Together with the muddy floor they spoke of a room left to its own devices, seldom stopped in, only hurried through to other, warmer, places, definitely the last on the list to be cared for. Miss Lamb aimed for a tall doorway past the staircase but Tibbs stayed put, defending his patch, barking at us as soon as we tried to follow her.

From inside the room a man's voice bellowed, "QUIET, TIBBS, QUIET!"

It was so loud it made me jump. I was already feeling on edge but the butterflies in my stomach grew to the size of bats. What if they didn't like us? What if they didn't like me? A grin spread across Arnold's face and he said quietly, "Best foot forward then, Zilla, here we go."

Chapter 2

Worry knotted my insides as we stood in the gloom and dust of the hall. I pulled off my gloves and straightened my back. Mum always said I should stand up straight when meeting people, she said, "You, Zilla Bunting, are just as good as everybody else so head up, my girl, and shoulders back."

Miss Lamb lowered her voice, "It is advisable in this house to knock on every door before you enter. One never knows what one might find. Always address Mrs Egmore as ma'am. She's very particular about it." Her knuckles rapped sharply on the door.

The arguing stopped and the man's voice barked, "Enter!" Tibbs barked back and the woman wailed, "Miss Lamb, keep that wretched creature out! I simply cannot bear the smell of it!"

"Sit, Tibbs, sit. Be a good boy and stay here," Miss Lamb patted his head. To give Tibbs his due he did as he was told. She pushed open the door and we filed in behind her, Arnold first and then me.

Mr Egmore came striding across the carpet to meet us, holding out his hand to Arnold, "Bunting, at last. So sorry Flack didn't meet you at the station. An oversight on my part I'm afraid. I was beginning to think you may have changed your mind and returned to Norwich."

"No, sir, we're here. Safe and sound," Arnold shook his hand eagerly.

Mr Egmore looked about the same age as Arnold, maybe thirty-three or thirty-four, but he was unkempt, even scruffy, and not at all what I was expecting. His hair was nearly down to his shoulders and his beard needed a good trim but there was kindness in his face that brought some relief to my strained nerves. I could see his clothes were top quality but they looked in want of cleaning. Small brown stains dotted the front of his waistcoat and his boots were caked in mud. He nodded towards me, "And what do we call you?"

"Zilla," I said, a bit too quietly.

The woman sitting in an armchair by the fire, who I assumed was his mother, let her embroidery flop onto her lap and said, "What was that?"

"Zilla," I said again, this time a bit too loudly.

Her pale, blue eyes looked me up and down and she groaned, "I suppose we must make do, mustn't we, Miss Lamb?" With her heavy neck and bulky body she put me in mind of an old toad laced into a corset. Her thick hair was looped up into a bun but at the back of her neck some of it had fallen out, trailing down the back of her dress. She tried to force a smile but it made her lips go thin.

Mr Egmore waved his hand in her direction, "My mother, Mrs Egmore."

"I'm sure if they have any intelligence at all, Charles, they will already have come to that conclusion." She picked up her embroidery again and stabbed at it with the needle.

"I daresay, Mother, but politeness costs nothing — even to staff!" The way they were glaring at each other I thought they were going to start arguing again in front of us but then she sneered slightly and said, "I wonder … Miss Lamb, what will Zilla's duties consist of?"

"The usual for a maid-of-all-work, ma'am — cleaning, washing, general housework and shopping."

"Does she … by any chance … have any ability with the culinary arts? … Cooking?" There was a desperate note in Mrs Egmore's voice. A wisp of hair fell across her face but she didn't seem to notice.

Miss Lamb peered at me, looking

hopeful, “Can you cook, Zilla?”

“A bit, ma’am. I helped Mrs Sowter, the cook at our last place, but it was food for the servants, ma’am, no fancy stuff.”

“Doesn’t have to be,” Mr Egmore said loudly, “just as long as it’s edible. Miss Lamb has many admirable qualities but unfortunately cooking is not one of them.” He laughed, a big booming noise to match his voice, “Perhaps you can come to our rescue.”

The thought of cooking for the gentry terrified me but I tried to sound confident, “Yes, sir, I’ll try, sir.”

“Good, good. Well then, Bunting, Zilla, I do hope you’ll both be contented here. Miss Lamb, will you be so good as to —” he waved his hand towards Arnold and me in the way that showed his thoughts had already moved on, “When you’re settled, Bunting, come and find me in the library.”

We’d been dismissed. Turning around we hustled ourselves out of the door, back into the chilly hall where Tibbs was waiting, still wagging his tail. “Good boy, Tibbs, good boy,” Miss Lamb patted his head and started walking back towards the front door, pointing out different rooms as her sensible shoes tap, tap, tapped across the floor, “There are eight bedrooms upstairs but only two are currently in use. This is the morning room. Not used now. Breakfast room, under wraps. Mrs Egmore's writing room, she seldom has any correspondence these days so she doesn't often use it."

A draught whistled from beneath the door and I caught a waft of something sweet mingling with the stale tobacco and cabbage, something completely unexpected, "Ooo strawberries!" I was so surprised the words just slipped out.

Arnold gave me his 'Be quiet, Zilla' look. Miss Lamb raised a quizzical eyebrow but didn't comment as she continued with her tour, "This is Mr Egmore's study. This room was used by Mr Henry Egmore, sadly no longer with us, but is still as he left it. Next we have the library. And this —" she opened the last door on the left, "leads to our part of the house." Arnold grabbed our bags and followed her through to a long, grey walled corridor, the black and red floor tiles covered in more of Tibbs' muddy paw prints. He padded comfortably along beside us. "As there are so few of us here the attic has been closed off. We always keep the door bolted. The stairs are in need of repair so for the time being we must all use the main staircase. Besides, it's so much warmer and more pleasant in this part of the house. Mr Bunting, I have put you in the butler's old room. I hope you'll be comfortable here," she pushed open the door. A fire was glowing in the grate, bed neatly made and not a single speck of dust lay on the polished top of the pine chest of drawers.

"I'm sure I will," Arnold was grinning from ear to ear as he carried his bag through the door, "very comfortable. Thank you, Miss Lamb."

"And you, Zilla, will be in the cook's old room," she opened the opposite door and my spirits lifted at the sight of it, "my own room is just along the corridor. Then there's the laundry, the scullery, the boot room, and last, but not least, the kitchen. I'll leave you to unpack. When you're ready come along to the kitchen. We'll have a cup of tea. I'm sure you must be in need of refreshment after your journey."

"Thank you, Miss Lamb, thank you!" The words exploded out of me I was so thrilled. A room, a whole room to myself. I'd never had a room to myself before and this one even had a fire in it. I waited until Miss Lamb was out of sight, dropped my bag, plopped onto the bed and bounced. The springs were a bit creaky but the mattress had no lumps in it and the quilt was beautiful, tiny diamonds of pink and red stitched together into stars that sparkled against a dark background. I pulled it up to my face, freshly aired, the warm scent of lavender lingered in the cotton. It took me less than a minute to empty my bag. On the top of the chest of drawers I stood the photograph of Mum, Arnold and me that had been taken on our last trip to Great Yarmouth, put both of my maids dresses and my skirt in the bottom drawer, blouses and nightdresses in the middle, foundation things in the top drawer with my other bits and bobs and the three bars of sweet scented soap that Mrs Sowter had given me as a leaving present. I was wearing my best boots so I put my working pair by the wall. A mirror hung above the chest of drawers and I took a quick look at my reflection and tidied my hair before I peeped around the door into Arnold's room. He was sitting on his bed, smug as Lord Muck.

"Not bad, eh, Zilla?"

"Not bad? It's wonderful. We've never had it so good."

"What do you think of Mr Egmore? He reminds me a bit of Lord Byron — you know — mad, bad and dangerous to know."

I shook my head, "Looks more like that

tramp who used to hang about the marketplace."

"Don't think he's that bad — sounded very considerate in his letters."

I laughed and looked along the corridor towards the kitchen, "Come on, I can hear the kettle boiling." Halfway along the corridor the acrid smell of burning reached my nose. As we got closer it mingled with the reek of boiling cabbage and by the time we reached the kitchen it was truly awful.

"Come in, come in. Sit yourselves down," Miss Lamb was almost lost in a cloud of steam as she poured boiling water into the teapot which, I couldn't help but notice, was chipped. She laid out three saucers then sat three teacups onto them before swirling the tea leaves around in the pot with a big spoon.

"I hope you don't mind my enquiring, Miss Lamb," Arnold sat down on one of the stick back chairs, "but why are there no more staff here? The house is far too big for you to manage alone."

"No, Mr Bunting. I don't mind at all. The question was inevitable. We had a full complement of butler, cook and kitchen-maid as well as two house-maids and a maid-of-all-work, however in the last few years all have left except myself." She poured a dribble of milk into the cups.

Arnold looked puzzled, "But the pay is very generous."

"Yes, indeed it is. Mr Egmore is a wealthy man and more than willing to pay well but the house has not been a happy one of late. Mother and son — let's just say that relations are somewhat strained. The butler retired and cook left to run a boarding house in Cromer taking both the housemaids with her," she poured weak tea into the first cup, leaving an inch wide collar around the rim, and started on the next. "Still, I'm sure Zilla and I will manage very well. Most of the house is under wraps and a man from the village takes care of all the maintenance tasks when needed." She put down the teapot and passed the teacups and saucers over to us, "Of course someone in the village is bound to tell you sooner or later so I'll tell you now — forewarned is forearmed — it wasn't just the lure of the bright city lights or better pay elsewhere that persuaded the others to leave. There was a bit of a scandal here a few years ago and no one wants to be tainted by association, if you understand me, so it's been almost impossible to find new staff." Arnold nodded sympathetically as she added, "But I'll say no more about it. Best let sleeping dogs lie." Arnold had said nothing about a scandal. I couldn't tell if he did know about it or if he didn't and was just nodding to be polite. Either way I knew that he wouldn't say anything about it in front of me even though I was certain I was old enough to hear it. I would have dearly loved to have heard a little bit of scandal — even a really big scandal. But instead Miss Lamb said, "You drink your tea. I must finish preparing their dinner."

She picked up a singed cloth to protect her hands, pulled an enamelled tray from the oven and put it on the table. Twelve sausages lay in it, smoking, their ends burnt black as charcoal. She looked perplexed. "It wasn't supposed to be ready until six o'clock but I can't seem to time the cooking correctly. No matter when I start no parts of the meal are ever ready at the same time. Either the meat is burnt and the vegetables are raw or vice versa." She sighed, "And sometimes all of it is burnt together."

A clock hung on the wall in the corner of the room, pendulum swinging as it ticked the minutes away. "I think you've started a bit early, it's not five o'clock yet." Our old cook, Mrs Sowter, wouldn't have fed those sausages to a dog but Tibbs sat up and started whining.

Looking totally defeated Miss Lamb

took a saucepan off the range and plonked it onto the table next to the tray of burnt sausages, "Of all the staff I miss the most I sincerely wish Cook was still with us. It's a skill I simply do not understand. I've told Mrs Egmore that I do not have the time to clean and learn the art of cooking. It's one or the other." She lifted up the lid. Inside a few lumps of potato floated in a lukewarm pool of white slush. "It's just as well no one comes to dinner anymore. Heaven knows what we would do."

"Would you like some help?" I felt compelled to offer.

Miss Lamb's face lit up, "Those words are music to my ears — more than you could possibly imagine."

"Have you got a colander?" She found one and, even though it didn't look as clean as Mrs Sowter would've wanted, I strained the potatoes and poured boiling water over the few lumps that were left to wash away the white slush. "If we mash them up with a knob of butter there'll be just enough for Mr and Mrs Egmore." I lifted the lid on the saucepan with the cabbage stewing inside it, just in the nick of time, a bit soggy but not totally ruined.

"They'll just have to eat early," Miss

Lamb put two plates onto a large silver tray.

"We can keep it warm while they dress for dinner."

"Good heavens — No! No, Zilla, there's no dressing for dinner in this house. I don't ring a gong either. They have to eat it when it's ready or not at all and as we have no one left to serve them I find it far more convenient to put it all onto plates. I do not have the time to clean all the serving dishes. Such are the circumstances we find ourselves in."

I was shocked but tried not to show it as I cut the burnt ends off the sausages before laying them on the plates. Next to them I put the mashed potatoes and tried to pat them into shape with a spoon so it didn't look quite such a mess before I strained the cabbage and laid it next to the sausages. Miss Lamb's gravy was her biggest disaster, thin and grey with big, congealed lumps that bobbed to the top as she poured it into the gravy boat leaving a slimy trail of gravy that looked as if a snail had crawled across the tray.

The sight of it was bad enough but the prospect of eating it was too much, "Perhaps we can have our sausages with bread as there are no potatoes left."

"An excellent idea," Miss Lamb placed

two silver, domed covers over the plates and picked up the tray. "There's some cherry cake in the tin on the pantry shelf. Do help yourselves if you're hungry and don't worry — it's quite edible. I didn't cook it. I bought it at the grocers. Peek, Frean and Company. They make such excellent cakes, don't they." She beamed at me, "Zilla, you're exactly what this house needs. I knew it as soon as I saw you."

I slipped a burnt end of sausage to Tibbs as we listened to the sound of her sensible heels tapping along the corridor. When we heard the door at the far end close behind her Arnold laughed, "Nice work, Zilla. Looks like you've got the cook's room and her job!"

Chapter 3

My first day's work and I'd overslept. What would Miss Lamb think of me! Pale light was just creeping in through the gap between the curtains as I grabbed my corset and petticoat. How could I have been so stupid? I yanked my dress over my head, tied up my bootlaces, grabbed my apron and dashed along to the kitchen expecting to see Miss Lamb but she wasn't there. It was empty. I felt like such a lemon standing all by myself in the half light, the only sound the tick, tick, tick of the clock. Quarter to seven. The old kitchen would be all hustle and bustle at this time of the morning. I thought of Nelly, Flo and Mrs Sowter, chatting while they worked, the room full of the smell of the master's coffee, bacon sizzling in the pan, bread toasting, and a lump came into my throat. We had only stayed there for six months but they had been so kind to me. My eyes stung as I blinked back tears but then something whacked against my legs and Tibbs woofed softly at me. I bent down and gave his head a pat, "Good boy, Tibbs, good boy. Now come on, Zilla, pull yourself together and get on with it." Sometimes I had to give myself a good talking to otherwise I'd start thinking about Mum and spend all day crying. I decided that if I got the fires going it would make a good impression, make up for getting up late. Not that Miss Lamb was aware that I'd got up late and I wasn't sure she'd have been that bothered even if she did know.

I lit an oil lamp and carried it through to the scullery. After a quick look round I found the ash bucket and a shovel but I could see no cloth to protect the carpet, no kindling or paper. Hoping that Miss Lamb would appear to give me instructions before I had to start on the fires in the family's rooms I got to work on the kitchen range, opening the fire box and riddling the coals. They were still smouldering so I cleaned out the ash box, picked out the small bits of coal that had fallen through the grate and put them back on the fire before I topped it up with more coal and left the dampers open to get a good draught through. The tap over the sink squeaked as I turned it. Icy cold water flooded out over my fingers washing off the ash dust, carrying it away down the plug hole with a gurgle. Mrs Sowter used to say that I could make tea in my sleep I was so good at it. The thought cheered me a little as I sat a kettle full of water on top of the range. There was still no sign of Miss Lamb but I thought that if I made a start on the fires I could always come back for kindling and paper if I needed them. A start would be better than nothing so I picked up the ash bucket and shovel in one hand, the oil lamp in the other and headed for the drawing room.

Tibbs followed with a reassuring snuffle. I was glad he stayed with me. The dark felt so heavy and oppressive as I crossed the muddy tiles of the hall, the smell of the previous day's burnt sausages and boiled cabbage lingered in the cold, still air. All the doors were closed, so tall they towered over me, their tops in darkness, the light from the oil lamp unable to reach them. There wasn't a sound. I fancied I could hear spiders spinning their webs in the dusty corners the silence was so intense and I didn't dare break it by knocking so I slowly inched open the drawing room door and peered in, worried I might be disturbing someone, maybe Mr Egmore was being mad, bad and dangerous to know in the dark, but the room was empty. Tibbs ignored my instructions to wait and followed me inside. I left the bucket and shovel by the fireplace and the oil lamp on the mantelpiece next to a half empty cup and saucer, tiptoed to the windows and pushed back the shutters. Condensation trickled down the glass. I thought it would be a relief to see the outside world but there wasn't much to look at, just a big lawn with some bare branched trees dotted across it and a dark hedge at the far side, beyond that dense woodland. The sky had lightened enough for me to see that we were under a thick layer of cloud. Yesterday's frost had vanished but I still shivered as I turned back to look at the drawing room. I'd been too nervous to take it all in when we first arrived. Two fine, dark sideboards stood against the far wall. Mrs Egmore's armchair faced a well stuffed, deep red settee on the opposite side of the fireplace. A small, round table standing next to the armchair was covered by a heavy tablecloth and on top of that nestled a host of little pots and boxes, embroidery silks and a pincushion. Between the windows a glass fronted cabinet held a collection of blue and white china that mingled with silver framed pictures. But when I looked more closely I could see the wear on the damask, the tea stains on the tablecloth, the dust on the mantelpiece. "Push off, Tibbs, you're not supposed to be in here," I growled at him as I knelt down but he shoved his face against mine and tried to lick my nose. Trying not to make too much noise I cleaned the grate. The fire had gone out in the night so I shovelled the ash into the bucket taking care not to drop any on the carpet and planned to come back later with paper and kindling. With my head so close to the ground I could see the dog hair covering the patterned carpet. A dropped teaspoon, bits of snipped off embroidery thread, pins, biscuit crumbs and a dead spider, its legs curled up, all must have gone unnoticed for weeks under Mrs Egmore's chair. Grate cleaned I picked up the bucket, shovel and oil lamp again.

Tibbs stuck to me like glue as we crossed the hall heading for the dining room. The family's ancestors, stern, old men dressed in grey, curly wigs and lace ruffs, looked down from the dark paintings on the walls as I drew back the curtains and got down on my hands and knees to get the fire going. As I stirred the glowing embers with the poker a draught whistled under the door bringing with it the sound of someone singing far off in another room, "Bye baby bunting, daddy's gone ahunting." The voice was distant, wistful, and a nursery rhyme seemed an odd choice of song. I paused for a moment to listen, guessing that it was Miss Lamb. The clock on the mantelpiece ticked the minutes away and I knew the kettle would be near boiling so I hurried with the fire. With the bucket full of ash and Tibbs at my heels I headed back across the hall towards the scullery to make another search for paper and kindling but as I walked past the door to Mrs Egmore's writing room I smelt it again, that lovely, sweet waft of strawberries. A wrong smell for the time of year it conjured up memories of roses and heliotrope, warm summer breezes, birds singing and I stood still, captivated, breathing it in, turning my face up to the daylight that filtered dimly through the misty glass above the front door as if the sun had just come out on a June day. I would have stood there longer but I heard a loud creaking on the landing and daren't linger for fear of Mr or Mrs Egmore catching me being idle. I hustled back to the scullery, washed the coal dust off my hands with a sliver of carbolic soap, dried them on the grimy towel that hung by the sink and stepped back into the corridor. Without warning, not even a knock, the back door at the end of the corridor flew open and a young boy shot in.

"Morning, miss," a blur of brown, curly hair and an outsized jacket he shoved the morning paper into my hands and was off again as if the devil himself was at his heels.

"Good morning, Zilla," Miss Lamb stood in the kitchen doorway, "that was Peter. He never stands still. That's as much as we ever see of him."

"I've got the fire going in the dining room, Miss Lamb, but I can't find any paper or kindling for the drawing room."

"It can wait," she held out her hand for the paper and I passed it over. I'd never heard anything like it, to even think that work could wait was, well, unthinkable. I was stumped. I didn't know what to do next. Steam hissed out of the kettle as she asked, "Would you like a cup of tea?"

I nodded, "Yes, please. But shouldn't I make it? Shouldn't I be doing something? Breakfast?"

"Heavens, no! Mr and Mrs Egmore don't rise until well after nine o'clock so we can take things at a more leisurely pace. We will have our own breakfast before preparing theirs. Now, I will make us tea. You will find bread in the crock and butter and marmalade in the pantry. Crockery in the cupboard over there," she pointed to the far end of the kitchen. I found a half empty jar of Golden Shred marmalade among the jars of jam sticking to the pantry shelf and a lump of butter freckled with breadcrumbs sitting in the butter dish. The bread was stale and had a bit of green mould on it but I rubbed it off and was setting it all out on the table when Arnold walked in.

He straightened his jacket, “Good morning, Miss Lamb.

“Are you sure I shouldn’t be doing something, Miss Lamb?” I asked, looking to Arnold to back me up but he just shrugged.

“No, no. Good morning, Mr Bunting. Do sit down, we are about to start breakfast,” Miss Lamb poured tea into three cups. Feeling awkward I sat down next to Arnold as she handed him a newspaper. I could see he wasn’t comfortable about taking it. The papers always had to be perfect at our last place. The butler would iron them so that the master didn’t get ink on his fingers. We wouldn’t have touched them before him let alone read them. But Miss Lamb didn’t seem at all concerned, “I don’t suppose this is what you’re used to.”

“No, not at all,” Arnold shook his head.

“This is a very informal house. Mr Egmore has thrown convention to the four winds. Mrs Egmore is not at all happy but just has to put up with it — and since the rest of the staff left us almost every vestige of the old ways left with them. But we muddle through.

He only has one rule — no alcohol."

"Don't worry, Miss Lamb, we've taken the pledge," Arnold reassured her as he buttered a slice of the dry bread. "We never touch alcohol. It's a temperate life for us. Mum made us both join the Band of Hope before she went so she knew we wouldn't get caught out by the evils of drink."

She took a sip of tea and laid the newspaper carefully on the table, smoothing it out, "I'm glad to hear it. Mr Egmore is very keen on self-improvement. We may be in the back of beyond but we should all endeavour to keep up with the times. There are so many exciting things happening in the world. But I do find it best to read the papers before Mr Egmore gets his hands on them. He cuts snippets out and keeps them. If I don't read them first I miss the most interesting bits."

"So what's the news today then?" Arnold smeared a thick layer of marmalade on top of his butter.

Miss Lamb perched her reading spectacles on the end of her nose and blinked twice, "I see that the Cullinan Diamond is to be presented to the King on the occasion of his sixty-sixth birthday. The largest rough diamond ever discovered, almost as big as a man's fist, it weighs three thousand one hundred and six carats." She adjusted her spectacles, "Well, I'm sure we would all like to be presented with one of those. It seems a little unfair, does it not, that someone as wealthy as the King should be given even more riches. If it were given to me I would sell it and I could do so much … make such a difference to the world."

'So could I,' I thought to myself as I tried to wash down another bite of the stale bread and butter with Miss Lamb's weak tea, 'I'd leave here for a start.'

Chapter 4

The frozen driveway had turned back to mud. Picking our way steadily between the puddles we reached the gateway at the end of the drive but instead of going the same way that Arnold and I had walked the previous day we turned to the right, following the road along the edge of the woods. Tibbs ran on ahead, nose down, sniffing all the way.

"The village is this way. You wouldn't have seen any of it yesterday," Miss Lamb strode vigorously along, basket in hand.

I had trouble keeping up with her, "Is it a big village?" I was hoping she'd say 'yes' but she shook her head.

"No. Church, school, public house, post office, grocers, bakers, butchers — the usual thing. But people are moving away to the towns and the factories — anywhere they can find more work, opportunities for a better life — and there's precious few of those on a marsh." As far as I could see there was precious little of anything on the marsh, just a scrubby green haze that covered it like a hairy carpet dotted with pools reflecting the dull, grey sky. Thick reedbeds fringed the creeks and gullies as they wound their way through the mud and far out on the horizon a thin line of steel grey. To my young eyes it was just acres and acres of empty, boring nothingness.

"Is that the sea, Miss Lamb?"

"It is. There's nothing but sea between us and the North Pole. I often imagine the polar explorers out there braving the elements. So very bold, so intrepid — I wish I were capable of such a thing." There was a note of frustration in her voice, "But we must each make the best of what we have." A long skein of geese honking wildly flew over our heads, gliding down from the clouds onto the far side of the marsh, disappearing into the scrub as soon as they landed. "Pink footed geese. They come every year to spend the winter here."

As she spoke we rounded a bend in the road, the woodland ended and the village came into view. I've never been so happy or relieved to see houses. Walls built from thousands of flint cobbles in every shade of grey, rooves bright with orange tiles, front gardens and backyards, privies and sheds, all squeezed cheek by jowl around a large triangle of grassy village green. And people, living, breathing people all going about their daily work. With everyone we passed we exchanged a polite, "Good morning," before commenting on the weather or some other pleasantry and as we left them behind Miss Lamb gave me their potted history. First old Mr Flack with his white hair and whiskery chin, widower, father of nine, five of whom are now in London, the youngest still works the horse and cart, lives in the last cottage on the track that leads to the marsh. Mrs Garnham, one child that died years ago and a husband with consumption, lives up by the school. Old Mrs Gibbs, almost bent double with a dowager's hump, had to turn her face sideways just to look at us, refuses to buy a new dress as she says the two she's got will see her out, and Mrs Pinch, harassed and careworn, with her two youngest children in tow, husband works away and sends her back money but there's never quite enough.

The bell jingled as Miss Lamb pushed open the bakery door and we were enveloped by the warm smell of freshly baked bread. "Good morning, Mrs Turner."

"Good morning, Miss Lamb. What can I get for you today?" Mrs Turner brushed her hands lightly on her white, floury apron as she stood behind the pristine counter, ready to serve.

"Two large loaves, please. We have new staff to feed. Mr Bunting, the librarian, and this is his sister, Zilla, who will be helping me from now on." Miss Lamb opened her purse and handed over her pennies.

"I'm sure we'll be seeing a lot more of you, Zilla." Mrs Turner passed the loaves across the counter, "Must be nice to have help after all this time, mustn't it, Miss Lamb?"

"Indeed it is, Mrs Turner, thank you. I've lost count of the number of times I've told Mrs Egmore that I only have one pair of hands so I cannot possibly do all the work required but now we have Zilla's hands as well, for which I am very thankful." Miss Lamb put the bread into her basket. Mrs Turner's round, pink face smiled but her eyes did not. They had a look in them. Worry. Mum used to have the same look every time Arnold went away, as if something bad was going to happen to him. As I closed the door behind us Miss Lamb said quietly, "She's charming but Mr Turner's an odd cove. Hardly ever seen in the village and his hands — they have the strength of the giant. It must be kneading all that bread."

Our next stop was the butchers. Tibbs sat outside and I wished I could have sat with him. I hate the smell of raw meat and the sight of the sawdust on the floor ready to soak up any spilled blood makes my flesh crawl so I was trying not to breathe too much or look down when Miss Lamb took me by surprise, "What shall we have for dinner?"

No one's ever asked me before. It was always up to the Mistress or Mrs Sowter to decide. I never had to think about it. So I said the first thing that came into my head, "Stew?" And then I thought that's not the kind of thing rich people eat but it was too late Miss Lamb had already asked for stewing beef and five pork chops for the next day. Mr Coe, the butcher, called through to his boy, "Ezra, you can drop this off at Creakie Hall for Miss Lamb on your way up to Mrs Norton's." He got no answer and rolled his eyes up, groaning, "That son of mine's away with the fairies. I've no idea what goes on in his head. Ezra! Did you hear me?"

Ezra wandered in through the doorway at the back of the shop, blue eyes, brown hair, a real chip off the old block in a bloody apron, muttering half-heartedly, "Yes, Dad. Creakie Hall. Miss Lamb."

In the grocers we were served by Mrs Bloggs. Tall, heavy and shapeless in spite of her corset, she packed the remaining space in Miss Lamb's basket with two tins of Carnation evaporated milk, a packet of Fry's cocoa, a packet of Fairy soap flakes and a jar of Golden Shred marmalade to replace the one we'd almost finished that morning. There was just enough room left for a new scrubbing brush, one I was fairly certain I'd be using. As soon as the basket was full she yelled, "LUCY!" Lucy dashed in like a startled rabbit, small and thin, looking no more than fourteen, eager to please, all nervous smiles and big green eyes. She hovered anxiously, waiting for Mrs Bloggs' instructions. "Two sacks of British Queen potatoes, two swedes, four pounds each of turnips and carrots, for Creakie Hall. Will's going up your way right now, Miss Lamb. Lucy, give him a shout quick. He can put them on the back of the cart." Lucy dashed out as fast as she came in. "On account as usual?"

Miss Lamb nodded, "Yes, thank you, Mrs Bloggs."

"Still cooking then?" asked Mrs Bloggs with a teasing note and raised her eyebrows enquiringly. She pulled a ledger from a shelf behind the counter, flicked to the right page and jotted down the amount spent.

Miss Lamb groaned, "Another disaster with sausages I'm afraid." Someone giggled behind us. "But now that Zilla has arrived we are all looking forward to a considerable improvement." I wasn't certain I could live up to her expectations so I said nothing.

A queue of women had built up while Mrs Bloggs had been serving us. I picked up the basket and was squeezing past them to get to the door when I heard a whisper, "It's not right. Someone ought to tell them." There was an awkward silence. Miss Lamb paused for a moment next to the unfortunate whisperer who lowered her eyes to gaze at the floor. Head up, back straight, Miss Lamb made her exit. As I pulled the door shut I took a glance back to find six pairs of eyes staring at me. Flustered, I spun away and nearly tripped over Tibbs who started yowling as if he hadn't seen us for weeks.

"I see word of your arrival has got round already. The gossips have been busy no doubt," Miss Lamb said a bit tartly. "Ignore them, Zilla, there's always somebody wanting to drag up the Egmore's past difficulties. I put it down to them having so little interest in the outside world they have nothing better to do but snipe at their neighbours."

"Yes, Miss Lamb," I tried to sound like I agreed with her but I was dying to ask what exactly it was I should be told about, what I should know, what was worrying the gentle Mrs Turner. But I knew better than to ask and kept my questions to myself. The clouds were threatening rain as we walked back along the road past Ivy Terrace, a row of flint and brick cottages each with its own neatly kept small garden. Before we reached the last one the front door opened up and a woman leant up against the door frame. “Morning, Miss Lamb. Suppose this is the new help.” I took a good look at her. Thick blonde hair swept up into a knot, about forty, small and dainty looking with a pretty face but her top lip carried a slight sneer. She wasn’t exactly common but had an air about her that wasn’t entirely respectable. I knew Mum wouldn’t have approved.

“Good morning, Mrs Pinkney. This is Miss Zilla Bunting. Zilla, this is Mrs Pinkney, who does at the Hall on Monday, Wednesday and Friday.”

“Good morning, Mrs Pinkney,” I hoped I sounded friendly because she certainly didn’t look it and I didn’t want to get off on the wrong side of her.

She looked me up and down, “Out from the city are we? Can’t think why you’d want to come here. Everyone except Miss Lamb wants to get away from the place. You must’ve been desperate.”

Her words threw me. I couldn’t think of an answer. Rattled, Miss Lamb retorted, “As I told you last week Mr Bunting is —"

But as her words tumbled out Mrs Pinkney turned a cold shoulder, "So you said, Miss Lamb. I'll see you on Monday." The front door slammed shut behind her. Through the window I saw a blonde haired child sticking its tongue out at us.

"Really!" Miss Lamb was steaming, her face bright red, "Good manners cost nothing."

I could see the neighbours' curtains twitch. They'd all have heard what was said, heard the door slam and seen us left standing there looking foolish. We walked briskly on, Miss Lamb muttering under her breath as she struggled to regain her composure. The sound of horses' hooves and the rattling of a cart distracted me and I looked over my shoulder, back towards the grocers. Leading the horse a man of maybe twenty-four or twenty-five years old called out to us, "Good morning, ladies."

Miss Lamb stopped, waited and I stood beside her, watching them as they drew level. Stinging from Mrs Pinkney's snub Miss Lamb spoke a little sharply, "Good morning, Will. Do you have our provisions?"

On Will's face a birthmark spread from his forehead halfway down his cheek. I tried not to stare at it but it was hard not to it was so deep red, so eye-catching. "Indeed I do, Miss Lamb. And this must be Zilla. We heard you and your brother had arrived." He tugged his forelock as if I was one of the gentry and I had to stifle a giggle. The horse came to a dead stop beside a gate. "He knows where we're going better than I do," Will chuckled as he walked to the back of the cart and hefted a sack of potatoes onto his shoulder as if it weighed no more than a sack of feathers. "Here, Zilla, give Duke this." He took a peppermint out of his jacket pocket and put it in my hand, "Keep your hand flat or he'll have your fingers." Keeping my fingers straight I put my hand under Duke's mouth. He snorted and sniffed, thick lips nuzzled my palm and the mint was gone. I tried to stroke his head but he jerked away, jangling the harness.

Miss Lamb was in no mood to dawdle as the clouds started spitting rain, "Come along, Zilla. We have no umbrella." She strode away. Tibbs was already far ahead, following his nose. The rain grew heavier, soaking the shoulders of Mum's black coat, splattering onto the muddy road as we marched on. The village and the woods behind us we'd almost reached the gates of Creakie Hall when we were overtaken by a woman on a bicycle, pedalling hard, green, purple and white ribbons flying from her wide brimmed hat. All thoughts of Mrs Pinkney forgotten Miss Lamb gazed admiringly at the cyclist as she crested the slope and sped away from us, “A suffragette! My goodness, a suffragette! Votes for women — I should say so!” But I had a different idea as I watched her disappear around the bend in the road. A bicycle, that’s what I needed. With a bicycle I could just ride away … maybe all the way to Norwich.

Chapter 5

Monday's always wash day. Wherever you live in the British Empire from the Australian outback to the African jungle to the tea plantations in India or Creakie Hall in Norfolk Monday is always wash day. I imagined all the women all around the world lighting a fire under the copper just as I had done at half past six in the morning, waiting for the water to boil and spending the day up to their elbows in soapsuds and all because it was Monday. I didn't mind washing my clothes and Arnold's. I was used to that. The soles of his woollen socks were all matted up where I'd darned them so often and when I soaked them in warm water they'd smell like old cheese. I could put up with that. But I didn't like the idea of washing Mr and Mrs Egmore's clothes, especially the intimate ones, his long-johns and her bloomers. I'd sprinkled Fairy soap flakes onto the warm water and was swishing my hands through it to dissolve them when Mrs Pinkney arrived. I didn't like her. I'd tried to but there was something about her, something hidden, secretive. She always spent the first hour of the day talking to Mrs Egmore instead of working. But she offered to take over, or rather, she offered an exchange of work, saying that if I'd scrub the hall floor she'd do all the washing. Relieved, I agreed, abandoning the packet of soap flakes next to the wash board and Mrs Pinkney rolling up her sleeves.

I took the stiff broom, a scrubbing brush and two cloths from the scullery and carried them through to the hall before I went back and filled up two buckets with water, pouring half a kettle full of hot water into each just to take the chill off. Standing in the gloom of the hall I tried to decide which mucky corner to start in, by the front door where it was lighter and I could see more of the dirt or under the stairs where it was darkest and get the worst part over first. I could see my breath it was so cold. A beetle scuttled along by the skirting board. I listened carefully for a moment, no one was about. Arnold was out with Mr Egmore and Mrs Egmore was in her bedroom so I opened the door to the drawing room to let a bit more light in, hoping some warmth from the fire would drift in with it. Bracing myself I gave the floor a really good sweep to get the worst of the mud off and then I knelt down in the corner under the stairs. Mrs Sowter had insisted that everything was done properly. I could almost hear her giving me instructions, “Dip your brush into the first bucket and give it a bit of a shake. Then scrub the bit in front of you. Scrub, Zilla, don’t just rub it about. Take the first cloth and mop up all the dirt, give it a rinse in the first bucket and wring it out. Now, dip the same cloth in the other bucket of water, wring it out and give the floor a good wipe to rinse it off. Now use the other cloth to dry the floor. We don’t want anybody slipping on a wet floor and hurting themselves, do we! Well done, Zilla, we’ll have you trained up in no time. You just keep doing that until you’ve finished the whole thing.” So I scrubbed and wiped and changed the buckets of water when they got too dirty until I could see the pattern of the tiles again, black and cream diamonds with a fancy border, and my hands were red raw from being wet and cold. Tibbs watched me, as bored as I was, both of us yawning the morning away.

The days ticked slowly by as I scrubbed and dusted and swept and slowly the shine came back to the house. But as is the way with housework the dust and mud came back as fast as I could clean it away and my work seemed endless. The evenings were as dull as the days. Sometimes Arnold would sit with us in the kitchen but mostly he stayed in the library. Mr Egmore said I could borrow any book I liked but most of it was about engineering, science and philosophy. I did find one book about biology that was useful. I knew that babies grow inside their mothers but Mum went before she had a chance to tell me how they got there and I felt too foolish to ask anyone at our last place. After reading that book the gap in my knowledge was filled and, as I'd often heard Miss Lamb say, forewarned is forearmed. The only novels in the library were by Dickens and I wasn't keen but I read them out of desperation and boredom. Miss Lamb spent most evenings sewing and helped me alter Mum's old coat. It had never fitted me properly but whenever I put it on and felt the shiny mother-of-pearl buttons slip between my fingers it was like Mum had her arms around me, that there was at least a little part of her still with me, keeping me warm and safe. Miss Lamb pinned and tucked and she may have been a dreadful cook but she would have made an excellent seamstress. Once it was a perfect fit it was no longer Mum's coat but mine and as much as I was glad that it fitted I was sad as well, another little piece of Mum had gone. When I wasn't cleaning I was cooking, peeling potatoes, carrots, swede, slicing ham, steaming fish and stewing beef. I knew my cooking wasn't as good as a proper cooks but at least it was edible, apart from one overambitious attempt at meat pie, and no one complained. After surviving on Miss Lamb's cooking for so long Mr and Mrs Egmore must have had stomachs of cast-iron and no sense of taste left at all. My cooking must have been delicious by comparison.

Miss Lamb was not a traditional housekeeper in any sense. She didn't carry the keys of the house on a chain around her waist, didn't rotate the linen to ensure that it was all regularly used and cared more that our quarters were kept clean and warm than the family rooms that Mr and Mrs Egmore lived in. Every morning she sat at the kitchen table with a cup of tea, perched her reading spectacles on her nose and read to me from the paper while I got the breakfast ready. All the latest news reached us from the far-flung corners of the world about explorations, inventions, rebellions, politicians and aristocrats, but more important to her than any of those were the suffragettes. Those courageous, campaigning women who marched with placards, chained themselves to railings, were sent to prison and went on hunger strike, all to get women the vote. And the woman she admired most was their leader, Mrs Emmeline Pankhurst of the Women's Social and Political Union. Pinned to the neck of her blouse Miss Lamb always wore a brooch in the suffragette colours, purple, for the royal blood that flows through the veins of every suffragette, white, for purity in public and private life and green for hope and the emblem of spring. She drilled into me until I knew it by heart.

I liked going shopping by myself just to catch a moment with Ezra or Lucy. Even when it rained I enjoyed the walk and walking, as Miss Lamb insisted, was the best possible exercise for a young woman to keep her fit, healthy and free from any feminine debility. Outside the house there was always the possibility of meeting someone new, a remote possibility admittedly but I kept hoping. I always dawdled on the way home, lingering for a few more minutes before I forced myself back inside the walls of Creakie Hall. Whenever Mr Egmore saw me coming up the driveway he'd open his study window, stick his head outside, looking slightly mad with his straggly hair and beard, and shout, "NO ALCOHOL?" And I'd call back, "No, sir, no alcohol." He spent most of his time with Arnold in the library studying his books or reading articles about the latest advances in science in the newspapers and periodicals. Most afternoons they went walking to post correspondence addressed to professors and doctors in universities all over the world. The post man brought him their replies but only he and Peter, the paperboy, ever called at the house and they never tarried, never passed the time of day. No wealthy ladies came to take tea, no cousins or aunts paid visits, no women from the village came to sit and chat with Miss Lamb in the kitchen so it came as a big surprise when there was a knock on the back door.

Ezra pulled off his cap, "Afternoon, Zilla. I was wondering like … you don't have to say yes … but I was just thinking … that if you like … if you're not too busy … you'd like to come for a walk … with me?"

I opened my mouth to say, 'Yes, absolutely, anything to get out of here,' but Miss Lamb had heard him from the kitchen where she was energetically cleaning a saucepan and called out, "Zilla, I'm quite happy to allow followers and you can take an hour off but I really think you should ask Mr Bunting's permission first."

"But Miss Lamb, Arnold's gone out

walking with Mr Egmore. I can't wait for him. They might not get back till tea time." Seized by a moment of boldness I added, "I can make up my own mind. I don't need his say-so. The suffragettes wouldn't ask him so why should I?"

Taken by surprise she stopped scouring and rolled her eyes up to the ceiling, "You modern young women! Always in such a rush." She wiped a cloth over the saucepan and waved me away, "Go on then. But don't be long! An hour — no more!"

A modern young woman. No one had called me that before. I liked it and I liked Miss Lamb all the more for saying it. "I've got everything ready for dinner and I'll be back soon — promise!"

"One hour, Zilla, and then you will be needed here and besides it's turned cloudy — it'll get dark early today."

Leaving the half peeled potatoes in their bowl I snatched off my apron and grabbed Ezra's arm, "Come on! Hurry before she changes her mind." I pulled on my coat, closed the back door and exhilarated by the mad moment of freedom we laughed together as we hurried along the driveway under the black, wind-blasted trees, "Where shall we go?"

Ezra grinned, "If we go to the village everyone'll be watching us — nosy old biddies. How about the woods?"

"Alright then, woods it is."

"Fancy a peppermint?" He pulled a paper bag full of mints from his pocket and held them out to me. I popped one in my mouth, hoping that he'd just bought them from Mrs Bloggs and they hadn't been sitting in his pocket for days.

A cold breeze bowled the dark clouds along until they joined together, smothering all the last fragments of blue sky. I turned the collar up on my coat and tried chatting as we walked along but Ezra didn't have much to say, just that he didn't want to be a butcher and when he was old enough he planned on going to the city to make his fortune. I wanted to tell him all about Norwich, about it being so lively with all the shops and the market but he didn't seem to be listening and I fizzled out. Neither of us said anything more until we reached the woods, following the narrow, well-worn path through the trees, their trunks strangled by dark green ivy, holding on as tight as any rope while the tips of their bare branches knotted into a twiggy canopy far above our heads. We went deeper. The breeze died away. The air grew colder. All was still, soundless.

"It's only another month till Christmas," Ezra broke the silence.

"I haven't got Arnold a present yet. I think I'll have to get socks. I can't darn his anymore — they're like cardboard." A twig snapped under my foot.

"It's my birthday on Friday."

"Really? How old will you be?"

"Seventeen," he smiled at me, "Give us a kiss, Zilla. For my birthday."

I hesitated. Armed with my new found knowledge that I couldn't have a baby by kissing I felt like giving it a try but I didn't like Ezra in that way. Then again he was the only boy who'd asked me and I wanted to know what it was like so curiosity got the better of me. I told myself it was just for his birthday and then I kissed him. Very quickly. It was over in a second. I'd like to say it was wonderful but it wasn't. Maybe it's because I'm strong and big boned but it didn't make me feel like the young women in novels feel. I didn't go dizzy or feel faint. He didn't seem to notice my feelings — or lack of them — and then he tried to put his hand on my backside. I wasn't having that!

I gave him a good, hard shove, "Get off! Keep your hands to yourself!" No hanky-panky. That's what Mum had said, "Zilla, my girl, no hanky-panky till you're married." She was gone but I wasn't going to let her down. I had no intention of ending up in the family way.

"Oh come on, Zilla, it's only a bit of fun," he tried to grab hold of me, "for my birthday!"

Mrs Pinkney's voice cut through the cold air, "You heard her, Ezra. Behave yourself." Caught unawares Ezra's face went as red as the blood on his butcher's apron. She stepped out from behind a nearby tree, "Hadn't you better get off back to the butchers? Your poor, old dad must be run off his feet. Big strong lad like you should be helping out your family — not spending your afternoon trying to ruin silly girls like Zilla."

He gritted his teeth, looked at the ground and avoided her eyes, "Yes, Mrs Pinkney." Then he shot me a dirty look, kicked angrily at the dead leaves and slouched away.

I watched him go, not saying a word. I knew I'd be in terrible trouble if she told Miss Lamb or Arnold or, worse still, Mrs Egmore. She tutted as she walked over to me, "Well, well, Zilla Bunting. So you're no better than you ought to be. You'll get yourself in trouble if you're not careful. Wouldn't be the first girl from Creakie Hall to do that. But don't worry … I won't tell."

Relief flooded through me, "Thank you, Mrs Pinkney." But when I raised my eyes to look at her I could see there was something wrong. Her blonde hair was loose, floating around her face and shoulders, her eyes were red, as if she'd been crying. Slowly she came closer until I felt her warm breath on my cheek. "I wouldn't have let him do anything," I blurted out, "I wouldn't! Really I wouldn't!"

"That's as may be but you've got a reputation to think of. Won't take much tittle tattle to lose that. Like I said I won't tell — but you'll owe me a favour for this and don't you go forgetting it. Now you get off home. Be dark soon and these woods are no place for a good girl after dark."

Nothing came free from Mrs Pinkney, no favours, no allowances, everything had its price and all debts must eventually be repaid. I made my escape back along the path, snatching a quick look behind. Standing all alone she was gazing at the emptiness between the ivy-covered trees, dead leaves stuck to the back of her coat. She'd been lying down. Who would lie down on the cold ground at this time of year I asked myself as I hurried away. I didn't want to stay in the woods, in the silence and the stillness and stumbled out of them onto the road but found I couldn't face going straight back to Creakie Hall either. The path on the opposite side of the road led down the steep bank onto the marsh and I wandered a fair way along it, waiting for my embarrassment to subside. In the vast, flat emptiness a bird was calling, burbling, the haunting sound carrying far over the miles of dreary scrub. Nothing moved except the water in the creeks, reflecting the dark clouds as it rippled between the mud banks. Then I saw him, a small boy standing by himself, far ahead of me. So pale with his blonde hair and white face that even from a distance I could see he looked ill. The light was just starting to fade and I felt a prickle of worry, he shouldn't have been there, all alone.

"Hey!" I shouted and waved, "Are you all right? What are you doing?"

His voice broke as it came back to me, pulled apart by a sudden gust of wind, "I'm waiting for my Mum." It was an odd place to wait. The sound of honking and cronking made me look up. Streaming across the sky in long V's, breaking and reforming, their wings beating hard, hundreds of pink footed geese started their long glide down onto the marsh, pouring in until the marsh was alive with their calls. One after another they flew in front of me. I looked around to see if I could spot the boy's mother anywhere but the only human souls were his and mine. Turning back to shout to him again, warn him against staying where he was, warn him of the danger, I found that he had gone. A shiver ran down my spine. Out to sea the tide had turned, water was pouring back in to fill the marsh's waterways, gurgling in the creeks as its flow quickened. I looked again, as hard as I could, straining my eyes to see him but he'd disappeared. Not wanting to leave him alone but not knowing how I could find him again I hurried back towards Creakie Hall. Drizzle fell from the darkening clouds turning the dry path slippery. My feet froze in my boots as I took one miserable, muddy step after another, determined that when I reached Miss Lamb I would tell her that there was a boy on the marsh. But as I trudged along he faded from my thoughts and they fixed on Mrs Pinkney standing alone in the woods, the distant look in her eyes, and the leaves on the back of her coat. She made me feel uneasy, made me feel that some things are best left unsaid. So I kept it all to myself and told no one about Ezra or her or the boy.

Chapter 6

Rain was sheeting down the next morning when Lucy knocked on the back door, water dripping off her hat and soaking through her thin coat. Miss Lamb pulled the door open squawking, "Don't just stand there, Lucy, come in, come in! You'll get soaked to the skin."

"Thank you, Miss Lamb, where do you want this? It's the Christmas bits you ordered. Mrs Bloggs said I was to bring it up right away — just like you wanted. She said all the orders have got to go out 'cos she don't want them cluttering up the store room," she held out the box, full with cake, biscuits and a box of chocolates. To my mind the box was far too small for a celebration.

"In the kitchen. Zilla will take care of it. Zilla, dry Lucy's coat by the stove and give her a cup of tea."

Lucy spun around, "Oh no, Miss Lamb, no, I can't stop. Mrs Bloggs wouldn't like it."

"I shall speak to Mrs Bloggs if she complains. You can't possibly go back out there in this. It's getting even worse. You'll catch your death." She was right to be concerned, rain was hammering against the window. “Now, sit down there and get warm. Zilla, the tea,” she reminded me briskly, “I’ll be cleaning Mrs Egmore’s bedroom should anyone need me.” And she left us.

Lucy smiled sheepishly at me as I passed a cup full of tea across the table to her, “Does Miss Lamb let you stop work?”

I nodded, “She’s very good like that. As long as I get all the work done she doesn’t mind if we stop for a bit.”

“Mrs Bloggs don’t let me stop. I have to have a drink on the move. I can only stop at midday for twenty minutes. ‘Just long enough to get some food inside you. We don’t pay you to do nothing,’ that’s what she says.” She took a mouthful of tea, “I’ve never been inside this house before.”

I was amazed, “What, never?”

“No, never. Mrs Bloggs says I’m not to. She says it’s a bad place,” she leaned towards me and whispered, “Mrs Pinkney says that Mr Egmore, with all his books and that, studies witchcraft and that people come in here and never come out. She reckons he could turn us all into toads.”

I burst out laughing, “Don’t be daft! He can’t turn you into anything.”

She looked a bit disappointed, “Nothin’? Nothin’ at all?”

"No. Nothing at all."

"I wonder why Mrs Pinkney said it then." She guzzled down the rest of her tea as if she expected Mrs Bloggs to suddenly appear and snatch it away from her.

I shrugged, "Just teasing I suppose."

"What's it like then — living here?"

"It's all right. Bit quiet, but it's all right. I'm getting used to it but I still miss Norwich."

Lucy's eyes widened, "Is it spooky? I saw a moving picture with a house like this. It was all dark and dirty and cobwebby … and there were ghosts and witches that jumped out at this girl dressed in white and she screamed a lot."

Having spent so much of my time cleaning so much of the house I was quite miffed, "It's nothing like that. Do you want to have a look?"

"Could I? Could I really? Won't Miss Lamb tell you off?"

"No. She won't mind," and I knew it was true. "Come on. I'll show you." She followed me along the corridor, past the scullery with its brooms and rags and ash bucket, the boot room with the blanket that Tibbs slept on, the laundry where Mrs Egmore's blouse was drying on the rack, past

Miss Lamb's room, Arnold's room and my room and the door to the attic that was always kept bolted. I opened the door into the hall and we both started to giggle like naughty children up to no good. I held my finger up to my lips, "Ssshhh." I could hear Mrs Egmore singing upstairs, which was unusual of itself, but I didn't want her to hear us. Unlike Miss Lamb she would view my giving Lucy a guided tour as outrageous impertinence. "Let's look in the drawing room first. It's empty."

Tibbs was stretched out in front of the fire. He raised his head then settled back down again, quietly shedding more hairs over the carpet to replace the ones that I had spent two hours cleaning away with a stiff broom, ignoring us as Lucy ran her hand along the back of the settee. "Isn't it lovely. Real posh. Mrs Norton's is posh but not as posh as this." She tiptoed over to the glass fronted cabinet, my favourite piece of furniture because the glass stopped all the china inside getting dusty, "Oooh, it's beautiful. Look — it's got little people on it."

It was my chance to show off a bit, "It's the willow pattern. It tells a story about a young man and woman who ran away from her dad to be together. He was so angry he chased them and they turned into birds and flew away."

I could see Lucy was impressed but my moment of glory didn't last long. Suddenly the door swung back and there was Mrs Egmore. I caught my breath, expecting her to lose her temper but she didn't, she swayed slightly and smiled her toady smile, "Aaah, Zilla, there you are. And you have a little friend … how lovely for you … I want your help. Come with me to my writing room," she waved a hand distractedly at Lucy, "you too, girl."

She wobbled as she turned away from us and Lucy whispered, "She's drunk."

I was amazed, "She can't be. Mr Egmore won't have drink in the house."

"Well she is. Drunk as a lord," Lucy giggled. I was so relieved not to have been sacked on the spot I had to bite my lip to stop myself laughing.

"Come along, Zilla. And you, girl," Mrs Egmore called from the hall. Despite her inebriated state she didn't slur a single word.

"Coming, Mrs Egmore," I called back and hissed at Lucy, "you've got to come too — you can't get out of it. She told you to." We hurried after her, forcing down another fit of the giggles, following her as she tottered slowly through the tall doorway into her writing room.

Her wobbles turned into a dangerous lean, "Catch her quick before she goes flat on her face," Lucy stuck her arms out to grab Mrs Egmore, catching one arm as I caught the other.

Mrs Egmore laughed, a frightening sound and not one I'd heard before, as she staggered towards a chair and flopped onto the seat, "What's your name, girl?"

"Lucy."

"Well, Lucy, what do you think of my writing room?"

Lucy took a long look around the room, "It's so pretty!" It was pretty, the prettiest room in the house. On the pale blue wallpaper small birds danced between finely painted leaves and flitted over pink cherry blossom that bloomed abundantly on long, curving stems. Gold framed landscape paintings of Italy and Greece basking under a Mediterranean sun were perfectly spaced to please the eye. The furniture was all so fine and delicate, made for a woman to sit on gracefully, and the french doors stretched from floor to ceiling with a view south across the lawn at the back of the house. When sunshine streamed in it would have been beautiful but the air was so damp and so cold and the rain was beating hard against the windows.

"I wish to see my mother's sapphire necklace," Mrs Egmore grabbed Lucy's arm as she lurched to her feet again and made her wobbly way to a painting hanging by the door.

Lucy tapped her own head and I knew what she meant, that Mrs Egmore had gone barmy but she hadn't. The painting wasn't hung but hinged against the wall and she swung it back to reveal a small, old safe. As she spun the dial on the front I smelt it again, that wonderful smell of strawberries, so wrong for the time of year. Lucy's face crumpled with anxiety, "I shouldn't be here, Zilla, I shouldn't know about this. I'll get into trouble. If Mrs Bloggs find out I could lose my place."

"Just don't tell anyone," I hissed back, "I won't tell — and she might not even remember."

"Ridiculous place to keep a safe. Every burglar — every sneak thief — knows they are hidden behind paintings. So stupid, stupid, stupid — but they wouldn't listen to me — nobody ever listened to me." Mrs Egmore rambled, "The number of times I've told

Charles — but will he listen — no — nobody ever listens to me." The safe door was loose, rattling and groaning as she pulled it open to reveal the Egmore's most prized possessions, bundles of envelopes and a stack of boxes. Rummaging clumsily through them she seized a long, thin ebony box, knocking the others onto the floor. Pearl necklaces, diamond earrings and brooches tumbled out, scattering over the carpet, and in the middle of the heap, one small, battered, square tin. Lucy tried desperately to prop up Mrs Egmore as she staggered back towards her chair, laughing as she clutched her prize.

I should have helped her but something stopped me in my tracks. It was the smell, the beautiful smell of strawberries that drew me to the tin box. And then, the deeper I breathed, roses, lilies, heliotrope like cherry pie, all mingling together with the warmth of summer. My hand reached down and just picked it up. The lid was loose and I found myself just sliding it off.

"Zilla," Lucy squeaked, "Zilla — What do you think you're doing? — Put it down! Come over here and help me — quick!"

But I couldn't put it down. I found myself slipping my fingers into the tin and taking out a small sketchbook. Dropping the tin I flipped back the cover of the book and the smell grew stronger, captivating, enchanting. Unable to resist I turned the first few pages, slightly damp but fine and velvety smooth between my fingers, blank apart from thin, pale grey lines, stains of images long since gone. The next page had a scratchy drawing of a goose in flight surrounded by words loosely scrawled. I only looked at it for a moment before I closed my eyes, drifting away on the delicious perfume, my mind lost in a summer haze so I didn't see what happened next. Lucy told me later. In the cold air she could see my breath leave my mouth. As it touched the book the ink began to move, slithering silently across the page. Lines trickled together, wriggling like fine worms as the ink seeped out from between the rest of the pages, oozing up and over their edges, forming a single black pool in the centre of the page that I held open. As my face drew closer to the book to inhale more of the scent the ink began to lift off the page, twisting and curling, rising up towards me as one long, fine, black ribbon. It tested the air, searching delicately, feeling its way, drawn to my warm breath until it found me. I didn't feel a thing as it slipped inside my nose, squirming its way into my head. Lucy watched, frozen, bewitched with horror, as it spread out underneath my skin until one eye and cheek and half my forehead were stained deep grey. As the last of the ink disappeared into my face something inside her snapped and she screamed out for help. Arnold and Mr Egmore ran in from the library and Miss Lamb clattered down the stairs.

The wonderful smell faded away and I found myself wide-awake, looking at their shocked faces, mouths open, eyes staring.

I suddenly felt ridiculous and laughed nervously, "What's wrong?"

I'll never forget Arnold's horrified expression as he asked me carefully and slowly, "You don't know?"

That's when Mrs Egmore raised her eyes to look at me, dropped her ebony box on the floor and screamed, "NOT AGAIN, CHARLES! NOT AGAIN!"

I stepped back in surprise, catching sight of myself in the mirror above the fireplace, "My face! My face! What's happened to my face?"

Mrs Egmore started to heave. Miss Lamb grabbed a fine china bowl from the table and stuck it under her chin just as she vomited, "Mr Egmore, if you could assist me we'll get your mother into the drawing room.

Lucy, Mr Bunting, take Zilla to the kitchen and keep her warm. Lucy, hot sweet tea, as quick as you can."

But Mr Egmore was unable to move, staring at me silently, utterly lost for words.

Sandwiched between Arnold and Lucy in that cold, damp room with the smell of sick in my nose and the sound of Mrs Egmore retching I began to shake like a leaf in a gale.

Chapter 7

Arnold stared at my face with horror, "And you really didn't feel a thing?"

I shook my head, "No. Nothing. Nothing at all."

Lucy stared at my face, her own as white as snow, "It just come up off the paper. Like a nose bleed going backwards — right up into your head. Horrible it was. Horrible!" Her hands shook so badly, striking the teapot against the cup, it was a miracle that she didn't crack the china as she poured the tea.

"Why didn't you try to stop me?" my hands were shaking as badly as hers and I slopped the tea from the cup onto the table.

"I couldn't, Zilla. It's like something froze inside me and then when I did shout at you it was too late 'cos it'd all gone up inside your nose and you didn't hear me anyway." She pulled a handkerchief from her pocket and wiped the tears from her red eyes, "It was like you was in a trance. Like at the Variety ... them hypnotists"

Arnold kept staring at me, thunderstruck, muttering, "Never seen anything like it. Never."

"And I doubt if you ever will again,"

Miss Lamb hustled into the kitchen, "Marsh Ink. Extremely rare. I thought it had been destroyed." She stared at me. They all stared at me. I put my hand to my face but I couldn't feel anything different. "How do you feel, Zilla? Are you in pain?"

"No … no, I'm not. It doesn't hurt at all."

"What do you mean — Marsh Ink?" Arnold frowned, "Destroyed? Why would it have been destroyed?"

Miss Lamb poured herself a cup of tea and sat down opposite me, "Not the ink exactly, Mr Bunting, more the book it was in. The book Zilla was looking at — I thought it had been destroyed."

"But why?" Bewildered, Arnold snapped, "What is Marsh Ink?"

"You need an explanation," Miss Lamb took a deep breath, "so I shall start at the beginning. Marsh Ink is not actually ink. It's a parasite that is found in the animals and birds that frequent the marsh — mostly geese but I did once see it in a piglet belonging to Mr Reece. It's said to float on the surface of the water, in a manner not unlike oil except that it's black and does look very like ink — hence the name. To the best of my knowledge it's completely harmless, unattractive certainly, but completely harmless. Mr Henry Egmore found some of this parasite floating in one of the pools on the marsh, presumably waiting for its next host. He had been out sketching and managed to trap it in an ink well by coaxing it in with a silver pen." As she spoke an image crept into my mind of a man leaning over me, his long, grey hair caught in the summer breeze, blue sky behind him, poking me with a silver pen and I felt a tiny twinge in my cheek as if the Marsh Ink was pained by the memory. She paused to sip her tea, "Sad to say Mr Henry Egmore would have been called the village idiot had it not been for his wealth and position in society. On his return home, either from forgetfulness or stupidity, he left the parasites in the ink well, added more ink and used it to make his sketches — if one could call them sketches — scribbles really . No one was aware of this until two years later when a young friend of Mr Charles Egmore was infected in the same way that Zilla has just been."

"Someone else was infected? Why didn't it infect Mr Henry?" Arnold's face was turning pink, bewilderment turning to anger.

"It prefers young flesh," Miss Lamb shuddered, "it's only ever infects the young. So Mr Henry Egmore was quite unaffected."

"But why wasn't the book destroyed then?" Arnold's voice grew louder.

"Please don't raise your voice at me, Mr Bunting," Miss Lamb's back stiffened. "I'm giving you an explanation. I am not the one who's at fault and to the best of my knowledge the book had been destroyed."

"But look! – Look what it's done to her!"

"SHUT UP, ARNOLD!" I didn't care about the book, "What about my face. I can't walk about like this. How do we get it out?"

Lucy began to sob again, already knowing what the answer would be. Miss Lamb paused, preparing to break the bad news, "I'm so sorry, Zilla, I'm afraid there is no way to get it out. It's inside you now and it's there for good."

My teacup shattered as I dropped it, "For good? Forever? But there must be a way to get it out! There has to be! I can't look like this for the rest of my life!"

"What about Mr Egmore's friend? What did the doctors say about him? What did they do?" Arnold's face was burning, steam coming out of his ears.

"I only know of two people who have ever been infected, both of them by the Marsh Ink in the book —" Miss Lamb stopped.

"What happened to them? I've got to get this stuff out of my face — I've got to! They must know what to do."

Miss Lamb reached across the table and held my shaking hand, "I'm sorry to tell you this, my dear, but they both died shortly after being infected so there wasn't time for the doctors to do anything at all. But they did not die because of the Marsh Ink — they died of completely unrelated conditions. Completely unrelated! Please do not fear on that account. It is absolutely harmless." Her reassurance was utterly wasted.

"Two?" Arnold raised his voice again, "Two? If two people have been infected why wasn't the book destroyed? Bad enough Mr Egmore's friend being infected but why was it left for anyone else to look at?"

"It wasn't left anywhere," Mr Egmore stood in the doorway. Miss Lamb, Lucy and I got to our feet but Arnold stayed sitting down. I didn't know how he could be so rude to Mr Egmore, even in the worst crisis every servant knows to stand up when the master comes in. "It wasn't left anywhere," he repeated, "the book was inside a tin, inside the safe. No one should have been able to get to it." He gestured that we should all sit down again, "It seems that even the best precautions can fail.

Perhaps I should have anticipated mother's actions but I did not. For that I am to blame. I am truly sorry, Zilla, that this has happened to you. I will do everything in my power to see if a cure is available. No stone will be left unturned. We will consult the best doctors and surgeons in London — in Europe if needs be." He came closer, his dark, unblinking eyes were unnerving, "How does your face feel?"

I shrugged, "Just as normal. I can't feel anything different at all."

"No pain? Is it still moving?" I shook my head. He turned his attention to Lucy, "What did it look like as it came off the page?"

"Like a ribbon, sir, a thin black ribbon waving in the air. Like it was searching about. It couldn't see her but it … well … maybe it could … smell her."

"You mean sense her presence?"

Lucy nodded and tried to avoid his gaze by looking down at the table top.

"Mr Egmore —" He waved Miss Lamb into silence.

"And did it move quickly? Or did it —"

Miss Lamb stood up, pushed back her chair and said firmly, "Mr Egmore really! That's quite enough questions for now. Zilla's had a terrible shock and she needs to rest."

"You're right, of course, Miss Lamb. Very thoughtless of me. Bunting, come to my study after you've attended to your sister and we will write to Dr Holman immediately. If he does not know what to do he may be able to offer some advice." Without another word he turned on his heel and stalked out.

More tears trickled from Lucy's red eyes, "I've got to go. Mrs Bloggs will give me hell when she hears about this. What if I lose my place? What'll I do?"

"Don't be silly, Lucy, of course you won't lose your place. I'm coming with you. I shall speak to Mrs Bloggs personally. This sort of news will spread through the village like wildfire but I'll see if I can't present the facts sensibly before the imaginations of the gossips get completely carried away. We must ensure that no blame is attached to Zilla in all of this. After all, she didn't open the safe."

Arnold nodded, "Thank you, Miss Lamb, thank you."

Miss Lamb guided Lucy towards the back door, picking up their coats and an umbrella on the way, "Another cup of hot, sweet tea for Zilla will do her no harm at all, Mr Bunting." She opened the back door, opened the umbrella and they both stepped out into the driving rain, "And you must stay with her until I get back. People in a shocked condition should not be left alone. Mr Egmore can wait an hour for his letter." The door clicked shut behind her and for a moment neither of us spoke. The sound of the rain hammering on the window filled the room. Somewhere in the hall Tibbs yowled. Arnold reached for the teapot.

"I don't want tea! It smells awful." With just the two of us there I couldn't hold the tears in any longer.

He put his arm around my shoulders, "I believe Miss Lamb when she says it's harmless but I'm sure we can do something about it. There'll be lots of doctors who can help you — bound to be! Modern medicine can work miracles. New discoveries are made all the time. We'll soon find a way to get rid of it — you'll see."

"Who's going to want me with a face like this?" I sobbed, "I wish Mum was here. She'd know what to do."

I felt Arnold's shoulder sag as I rested my head against it. He pulled a handkerchief from his pocket, "I wish she was here too but she isn't. We'll make the best of it. We'll manage somehow, you'll see. We'll have you back to your old self in no time!"

By the time Miss Lamb returned both

the shoulder of Arnold's jacket and his handkerchief were soaked with my tears.

Chapter 8

As soon as Miss Lamb opened the back door, before she'd even finished shaking the rain off her umbrella, Arnold stood up, "Right, I'm going to see Mr Egmore. I'll sort this out."

I knew what Arnold was like when he got a bee in his bonnet, never knew when to stop, "Don't say anything silly. We can't lose our places. We've got nowhere else to go."

"I know. I know. I'll be reasonable. You just stay here and rest." Chin set, back rigid, he left the kitchen.

I groaned, "Oh no. He's going to lose his temper — I just know he is."

Miss Lamb picked the cake tin off the dresser shelf, "Don't distress yourself, Zilla. Mr Egmore has heard far worse from his own mother than anything your brother could ever dish out and, to be honest, I agree with Mr Bunting. Keeping that book was an act of pure stupidity. If Mr Bunting tells him so then I think he deserves it. Would you like another cup of tea?"

"No, thank you," the last thing I wanted was another cup of tea. It smelt awful, harsh and strong. I tried not to show my disgust on my face, but I was never much of an actress.

"You don't like it anymore do you?" I shook my head. "Perhaps you'd prefer this," she pulled the lid off the cake tin and the sweet smell of cherry cake wafted towards me. I nodded and blew my nose on Arnold's soggy handkerchief. "Ada hated tea after she was infected. She'd only drink milk and honey — or plain water."

"Tell me about them, please, Miss Lamb. About the others."

She cut a large slice of cake, plonked it onto a tea plate and pushed it across the table towards me, "Eat this. You must keep your strength up. It'll make you feel better."

"But I don't feel ill. Tell me about them … please."

"Only if you have a mouthful." I took a bite and chewed it slowly. "Ada didn't feel poorly either. Not a single day of sickness after she was infected, dear girl. Neither did little Tommy Cottle." She cut herself a slice of cake and took a mouthful. She would never be rude enough to talk with her mouth full so I waited until she was ready to speak again, "Mr Henry Egmore had a profound misunderstanding of the boundaries of class and encouraged his son in an entirely unsuitable friendship with Tommy. They were such chums — two peas in a pod. One day they were playing hide and seek and Tommy ventured into the study where Mr Egmore was asleep with the book in front of him on his desk. He said later that the smell of strawberries had enticed him into the room — not everyone can smell it, you know. The ink rose up off the paper and infected him the same way it has infected you. Mr Egmore woke to Charles's cries for help but I'm afraid Tommy had already inhaled about three pages worth before Mr Egmore was able to intervene. He suffered terrible guilt, which didn't help his mental condition. It happened twenty-five years ago. I can remember it as if it was yesterday." She stopped again and took another mouthful of cherry cake. I listened to the rain beating against the kitchen window as she ate.

"Is that when he died … Mr Henry Egmore?"

Miss Lamb looked around the room as if she was expecting eavesdroppers to be lurking in every corner before she leaned across the table and whispered, "In strictest confidence, just between you and me, Mr Henry Egmore is not dead. He was committed to a lunatic asylum in Bristol. As far away from the family as they could get him. Mrs

Egmore couldn't cope with his behaviour and the shame of it — well, as far as everyone else is concerned he's dead."

"Everyone? Doesn't anyone in the village know?"

"No. And it's staying that way. They said he was paying a visit to family in the West Country and died after a riding accident." Another mouthful of cake, another wait, "Of course that's why they're stuck here now. Legally Mr Henry Egmore still owns the house so Mr Charles Egmore can't inherit until he really does die. If they did try to sell questions would be asked and the truth would inevitably come out." The sound of Arnold's raised voice reached us from the hall, "I think your brother is telling Mr Egmore his fortune!" Miss Lamb tried to smile, "At least they can't disturb Mrs Egmore. She'll be comatose until at least six o'clock. Now, Zilla, I really think that you should go to your room and lie down. At least for little while. I'll make luncheon and you're excused duties for the rest of the day so I'll cook dinner as well." Doubt crossed her face, "Perhaps only sandwiches for luncheon."

But I didn't want to go to my room. A mirror hung above the chest of drawers and I didn't want to see my reflection, to see the change. Maybe if I didn't look at the Marsh Ink it would, in some mysterious way, disappear. The back door flew open, banging as the handle hit the wall, and Mrs Pinkney rushed in, pink cheeked and breathless. She tossed her umbrella onto the floor and came straight to me, standing over me, staring down at my face, "So it really has happened again then?"

"The village gossips have already started work have they?" Miss Lamb said tartly.

"I couldn't believe it when I heard. Had to come and see with my own eyes," she reached out to touch my cheek. I pulled my head away and her hand dropped down by her side. "They should have burnt that bloody book. Burnt it long ago. Killed poor little Tommy it did. Sure as there's blood in my veins that's what did for him."

"Now, now, Mrs Pinkney. We all know it wasn't the Marsh Ink at all. It was tragic but it wasn't the Marsh Ink. And we mustn't alarm Zilla. She's had quite enough distress for one day," Miss Lamb got to her feet and began to bustle around the kitchen, tidying away the empty cups and saucers, putting the lid on the cake tin, fussing with things that didn't need doing.

I didn't like the way Mrs Pinkney kept staring at me. She backed away a little but her eyes remained fixed on my cheek, forehead, eyes and there was a sadness in her face that reminded me of the way Mum used to look at me when she knew she was going. I was suddenly filled with a desperate need to be on my own, to get away from their stares, "I think I will go to my room after all, Miss Lamb. Perhaps I do need to lie down."

"Very sensible, Zilla. Now Mrs Pinkney is here I'm sure she'll be able to assist with preparing luncheon — and possibly dinner."

Mrs Pinkney's eyes were still fixed on me as I left the room but once in the corridor it took every ounce of strength I had to keep walking. Tibbs had been lying behind the hall door and was on his feet as soon as he saw me, padding quietly along the red and black tiles. His smell, which had always been rather strong, had softened somehow, had become less offensive. I closed my bedroom door, shutting everyone out, and sat down on my bed. It was reassuring to have Tibbs with me. He didn't stare, didn't ask questions and I stroked his fluffy ears until I felt calmer and braver, brave enough to face the mirror. I knew I'd have to. When I couldn't put it off any longer I took a deep breath and stood up.

Four paces. That was all it took to cross the room, my eyes fixed on the top of the chest of drawers. I leant on it for support as I raised my head and looked straight into the mirror. My right eye, cheek and forehead were dark grey where the Marsh Ink had settled under my skin. I reached up and prodded it, expecting it to hurt or the ink to move, but nothing happened. Nothing felt different. It was just a different colour. Grey where it should have been pink. For a long time I stood and looked at my reflection while the rain hammered relentlessly against the window and the draught whistled under the door.

"Well, Zilla Bunting," I whispered to myself, "you've done it this time."

Chapter 9

I slept like a log. Even Miss Lamb's brave but undercooked attempt at beef stew didn't give me indigestion. Watery light washed through the gap in the curtains. The room was cold. The fire in the grate had gone out overnight. Not wanting to face the day ahead I snuggled down under the covers longing for just a few more minutes when I heard footsteps in the corridor. Miss Lamb, probably. I felt my face. No change. Just the same as it had always felt. Half of me knew that when I looked in the mirror the Marsh Ink would be there and the other half desperately hoped it wouldn't. But the minutes were passing so I dragged myself from between the warm sheets, pulled on my clothes and braced myself to look in the mirror. It was still there. An ugly patch of dingy grey. I knew I wasn't beautiful but now I was marked for life. I wanted to lay down on the bed and howl, sob until I couldn't sob any more. But you can't cry forever. I found that out when Mum went. Sooner or later you have to take a deep breath and carry on so I swallowed the lump in my throat, wiped my eyes with the back of my hand, opened my bedroom door and stepped out into the corridor to face the day. Silence. Nobody there at all. No sign of Miss Lamb or Arnold. The hairs on the back of my neck stood up as the sound of singing came from the kitchen. A mysterious, thin voice singing, "Bye baby bunting, daddy's gone ahunting." It didn't sound like Miss Lamb. Maybe it was Mrs Egmore, maybe she was looking for more drink. Hoping to avoid her I crept along the corridor and peeped through the kitchen door. Empty. Not a soul was there. I ran my hand along the top of the stove. Stone cold. The chairs were neatly tucked under the table. Last night's cocoa cups stood in the sink. Miss Lamb's sewing box stood on the dresser where she'd left it. The kettle was empty. The clock ticked on. I was the first up. But as I stood by the sink something touched my arm, something cold — fingers, icy cold fingers. My skin prickled with goosebumps. My stomach tensed. My heart thumped, "It's nothing, Zilla," I told myself, "stop imagining things." Footsteps again. But this time behind me. I held my breath, not daring to look. A hand touched my shoulder.

"Good morning, Zilla."

I spun round and found myself face-to-face with Miss Lamb.

"Goodness me, you're very jumpy this morning. Did you have a bad night?"

"No, Miss Lamb, no I didn't. Thank you," my stomach slumped with relief, "I thought I heard someone singing in here."

She bustled past me, "No one here but us. Your nerves are probably still on edge. A nice hot drink will calm them down." Picking up the kettle she said, "You must go shopping this morning. You have to face the villagers and the sooner you do it the better."

My poor stomach turned over again, "Do I have to? Can't I wait another day?"

The sound of the tap running almost drowned out her voice, "No, you must go today. But have no fear — I shall be coming with you. I wouldn't expect you to face them alone." It didn't do much to reassure me but it would be a brave soul that took on Miss Lamb when she had her dander up.

The clock was striking ten as we closed the back door and set off along the driveway at a smart pace, Miss Lamb tapping the ground with the tip of her umbrella every step of the way. Neither Mr nor Mrs Egmore were up so Arnold was left to make them tea and toast and 'Hold the fort', as Miss Lamb put it, until we got back. Thick cloud hung over the marsh, promising rain later in the day, but my heart lifted to be out in the fresh air, fresher than I'd ever known it. It was an odd sensation but it was as if the Marsh Ink felt happy, happy to be free from the pages of the book and living again, and its happiness spread gently through me, blotting out a little of my misery. But then we reached the village. Men and women, boys and girls, the old and the young, they all stopped what they were doing and stared at me as we walked past. Miss Lamb said, "Good morning," relentlessly but no one answered her. They stood in a strange, fascinated silence, neither hostile nor friendly, all eyes fixed on my face. My cheeks burned red. At least one did — the other stayed grey. At the butchers my stomach churned, the smell of blood and raw meat so disgusted me that I thought for a minute I would be sick. Ezra was nowhere to be seen. Mr Coe, who was normally so chatty, ignored me completely, wrapping the sausages and beef in paper and handing them to Miss Lamb with barely a word, only mumbling, "Thank you," when she paid him.

She was still bristling with anger and I was still feeling queasy as we walked into the grocers. Lucy, fluttering like a tiny bird, opened her mouth to speak but snapped it shut as Mrs Bloggs ordered her to, "Get out the back, Lucy! Go and sweep up."

"I'm now going, Mrs Bloggs, I'm now going," Lucy squawked, scuttling away into the back room.

Mrs Bloggs glared at us across the counter as, item by item, she filled our basket. Cherry Blossom boot polish, Pears soap, two packets of Lipton's tea, with every item her scowl grew deeper. Behind us I could hear breathing, feet shuffling, skirts rustling, as the shop filled up. We turned to leave and were confronted by a mass of faces, all staring, all curious, all silent.

"Good morning, everybody. Come along, Zilla, we have work to do," Miss Lamb's straight back didn't flinch and the onlookers parted, squeezing themselves away from me as if fearing infection by the Marsh Ink if they stayed too close. Outside Miss Lamb said quietly, "Head up, Zilla, don't let them intimidate you." Gasping for air I tried but my eyes kept going to the ground, anything to avoid them all. Desperate to get away I tried to hurry but Miss Lamb maintained her steady pace.

"MISS LAMB! A word if you please," Mrs Bloggs had left her place behind the counter and was pounding along the road behind us.

"Mrs Bloggs. Is something amiss?"

"You know full well it is!" Mrs Bloggs' beady eyes fixed on me. She put her hands on her shapeless hips. Miss Lamb's shoulders went rigid. The two of them were like prize fighters sizing each other up. "Don't send her here again," Mrs Bloggs' thick finger stabbed the air in my direction, "I won't serve her and I won't have her in my shop. I represent the villagers and they don't want her here. Not anymore. Not with that stuff in her face."

Miss Lamb brandished her umbrella, "That is totally unreasonable. Zilla has done nothing wrong and as everyone knows Marsh Ink is completely harmless. She cannot infect anyone else. No one has anything to fear from her!"

"That's as may be. But it would be far better for everyone if she left here. It's for her own good! And you know it!"

"Mrs Bloggs, this is outrageous!" Miss Lamb stuck her chin out but Mrs Bloggs was the taller of the two and glared down her nose at Miss Lamb.

She had the upper hand and she knew it, "Do not send her here again. We are all in agreement, Mr Coe, Mr and Mrs Turner and myself, we won't serve her. And the villagers don't want her here. This kind of thing isn't good for the nerves of decent folk. We don't want strangers turning up trying to cut it out of her — doing all sorts — none of us will talk to them and none of us will talk to her neither — none of us. So there you have it!" She looked daggers at me, "Time to move on, young lady, and the sooner the better!" Turning her back on us she marched back towards the small crowd that stood gawping.

"Come along, Zilla," Miss Lamb knuckles were white as she gripped her umbrella handle. She almost exploded as we stormed past the end of the village green, every step of the way stabbing the road with her umbrella, "HOW DARE SHE! How dare she! The narrow minded — bigoted — ignorant — that woman is as stubborn as a mule! All the years the Egmores have patronised her business — spent good money in her piffling little shop! Representing the village indeed! She's nothing but a loudmouthed bully. I can guess who put her up to this. I don't suppose anybody else had a choice in the matter!" The tirade didn't stop as we passed Ivy cottages and I caught a glimpse of Mrs Pinkney twitching her curtains, a wisp of blonde hair and a smirk. "Did you see that?" Miss Lamb snapped as she stormed on, "I'll find out if she's behind this, you see if I don't. Cleaner? — She couldn't clean a house properly if her life depended on it." By the time we reached the gateway to Creakie Hall her anger was almost burnt out and we slowed to a steady walk. She stopped and put the basket down. "If there were any other shops near enough I would go to them and tell Mrs Bloggs and the others exactly what I thought of them. I'd take our custom elsewhere but there are no shops. Its four miles to town and I can't walk that every day. I'm sorry, Zilla, it seems our choices are limited. In fact, we haven't got a choice at all."

Rain drizzled. Miss Lamb opened her umbrella and held it over both our heads. I picked the basket up but I couldn't think of anything to say that would make either of us feel better so I said nothing as we started walking again, picking our way between the muddy patches. As we drew near the house the spots of rain grew heavier, falling steadily and I wished for all the world they could wash away the Marsh Ink. A white face topped with wet, blonde hair peeped timidly out from behind the trunk of one of the black, wind-blasted trees. The same boy I'd seen on the marsh. I was about to point him out to Miss Lamb when I thought better of it. Another pair of eyes gawping at us would only fuel her anger. His mouth widened into half a smile as we went past. Half a smile that morning was better than none at all.

Mr Egmore distracted me, shouting from the study window, "NO ALCOHOL?"

I left Miss Lamb to answer him and looked back towards the boy but he had gone, vanished into the morning gloom.

Chapter 10

Carrying a basket full of logs I hurried through the gloom of the hall and knocked on Mr Egmore's study door. "Enter!" he barked from the other side.

"Just come to do the fire, sir."

Sitting behind his desk he was almost lost behind stacks of papers and books. Mr Egmore was a man of contradictions. As much as he was scruffy in his clothing, it was always mucky and he always left a trail of it across his bedroom, when it came to the things he valued he was meticulously neat. Everything in his study had its place from the books on the shelves arranged in alphabetical order to his collection of rocks and minerals, all neatly labelled. He didn't speak but waved his hand in the direction of the fireplace and I set to work with the poker. I'd barely got started when his muddy, brown shoes appeared next to my knees, "Zilla, stand up!"

"Why?"

"Just do as I ask."

He put my nerves on edge. I laid down the poker, wiped my hands on my apron and stood up. Not wanting to look directly into his eyes I stared at the watch chain hanging between the pockets of his waistcoat and waited. Without warning he lunged forward, grabbing the back of my head with one hand and pushing something hard into my cheek with the other.

"OOOWW!" A sharp pain seared through my cheek.

He let go of me and took a step backwards, waggling a silver spoon in his hand, "Fascinating."

I held my poor face with both my hands and tried to rub the pain away, "What did you do that for?"

"I wanted to see how sensitive to silver the Marsh Ink really is. In his last days Father claimed it was repelled by silver. Ada wouldn't let me examine her face so it was impossible to ascertain if he was correct. He was. Quite surprising." Pleased with himself, he smiled and lifted his hand to my cheek again. I jerked my head back to get away from him. "Don't be frightened. I won't use the spoon again." My hands dropped and I let him prod my cheek with his fingers, "Take a look in the mirror."

I'd been trying to avoid every mirror in the house since I'd been infected but now I had no choice. I raised my eyes to look in the mirror hanging above the mantelpiece. My stained face looked back at me but the Marsh Ink had moved. In the centre of the grey patch an area the size of a one penny piece, where Mr Egmore had pressed the spoon, was pink again, the same as the other cheek, the same as it used to be. I touched it with my own fingers, still smooth it felt no different, but as I stared at my reflection the Ink began to move, filling the space again and my cheek turned back to grey.

Mr Egmore bent his head for a closer look. His breath smelt of tobacco and coffee, "Most fascinating. It appears it can be driven from one particular spot by the use of silver but whether it would be possible to drive it out of a body completely I couldn't say. I presume it would go deeper to some internal organ and remain there. My apologies for inflicting discomfort but I thought if you knew what I was about to do you may have been afraid. Your emotions may in some way be transmitted to the Marsh Ink and then its reaction would be altered … prepared … forewarned."

He was so close I could see the many small stains that dotted his waistcoat and a few crumbs in his beard from his morning toast. I blurted out, "Sir, can I ask you something?"

He raised his eyebrows, "You may."

"Why didn't you burn the book? Why wasn't the Marsh Ink destroyed after it infected the other two?"

"It didn't hurt them. It would be rare for a parasite to kill its host. It would kill itself in the process," he walked away from me and sat down behind his desk. "They both lived with it just as the birds do on the marsh. I'm in agreement with Miss Lamb on this point — we don't believe it was the Marsh Ink that killed them. But as for burning the book," he leaned back in the chair and said bitterly, "money. The root of all evil."

"Money?" I didn't understand, "who'd want to pay for Marsh Ink?"

"You'd be surprised. The book — or what was left of it — was probably the most valuable object in the whole house." I felt a twinge of guilt. It hadn't occurred to me that the book was worth anything. His face softened slightly as he guessed what I was thinking, "Don't concern yourself about it. It was also the object I hated most. Had it been burned as suggested or had the tin been airtight so that the scent of the Ink had not captivated your attention you would not be in your current condition. But as you have been — invaded — we have a duty of care. We must do what we can to make amends." He tossed the silver spoon into a dish next to his microscope, "I've seen illustrations of ants in the tropics that lock their bodies together so tightly they form a living bridge for the rest of the colony to safely cross from one place to another. I think that the Marsh Ink is similar. The vapour from your breath combined with the dampness of the room allowed it to become mobile again. Although each tiny parasite is almost invisible together they can form a moving ribbon to hunt out their next host. Some people, scientists, doctors, think that it would be possible to use the Ink as a means of carrying other substances into the body."

"You mean like medicine?"

"Medicine? Possibly." He flicked the papers on his desk, "But more likely poison. Send your enemy a letter and the intoxicating odour of the ink will entice them to inhale the combined ink and poison all by themselves. It has been pointed out that the Ink only infects the young but some think that this aspect of its behaviour could be overcome. The ability to kill from a distance and leave no trace, many would pay dearly for such a thing. So, do we sell it to them — give them the means to commit murder and make ourselves a fortune in the process? Do we destroy it? Or do we keep it in the hope that one day we may be able to analyse it and improve our knowledge of the world?"

"Murder. That's not very nice."

"No. I would say it's extremely unpleasant."

Mrs Bloggs suggestion that strangers would come to the village and try to cut the Ink out of me had been preying on my mind, "Sir, what do you think these people will do if they find out that the Ink is all in my face? Will they come here? What if they try to cut it out of me?"

"I for one will never reveal to anybody what has occurred and neither will anybody in the village. They have a natural distrust of strangers and if Mrs Bloggs has instructed them all to keep silent — then silent they will keep." He picked a book off the desk, stood up and strode towards the door, "The world is not always a pleasant or friendly place and some of the people in it are most repellent but I believe you're quite safe for the present."

Left alone in the room I looked into the mirror again. The pain had gone, the Marsh Ink was back in its usual place and I had been offered a glimmer of hope that maybe one day it would be gone. I stared at my reflection, the pink and the grey, and, strangely, the longer I looked at the Ink the less troubling I found it. Fifteen minutes must have passed before the sound of footsteps clipping on the hall tiles brought me back to my senses. I knelt down and picked up the poker when a cold draught blew under the study door. Chills ran up my spine as I heard a singsong whisper, "Bye Zilla Bunting."

Chapter 11

Two days had passed since Mr Egmore's experiment with the silver spoon and the Ink hadn't moved again but no allowances were made for having a face infected with Marsh Ink and nothing stopped the daily grind of my work. I slid my duster along the mantelpiece in the drawing room, carefully lifting up each trinket, wiping underneath it before putting it down again. Mrs Egmore was bound to check that it had been done properly, which I thought was a bit rich bearing in mind how grimy it all was when we'd arrived. When sober she was finicky, everything had to be just so, perhaps in the hope that one day some wealthy lady would call on her and she would be ready for inspection. But Mr Egmore made a mess everywhere he went. Discarded pages of newspapers with the interesting bits neatly clipped out littered the route from the study to the library, an ink pen was left to stain the expensive fabric covering the chair in the hall and his wet, muddy socks were abandoned along the landing.

The front door slammed behind Mr Egmore, Arnold and Tibbs as they left for their afternoon walk, promising muddy paws and muddy boots two hours later. As I watched them walking down the driveway I heard someone singing. Duster in hand I followed the sound, across the hall, along the servants' corridor, stopping by the door to the attic stairs. Although still faint the voice was louder than before. Someone was up in the attic. The attic door was a barrier I had never crossed. Miss Lamb had told us that the stairs were in need of repair so we always used the main staircase. But the bolt had been slid back and spotting Mrs Pinkney's coat hanging on the pegs by the back door I asked myself, 'What's she doing up there?' Curiosity led me on. Gently, quietly I opened the door and sneaked, step by step, up the stairs. The wooden treads looked in perfectly good condition apart from a layer of dust so thick it had not been disturbed by Mrs Pinkney's feet. The smell of old plaster, musty and damp, hung in the clammy air like a heavy fog. Distemper flaked off the walls. "Bye baby bunting, daddy's gone ahunting," the singing was louder, clearer but still slightly muffled. At the top of the stairs the landing stretched out straight ahead of me. On either side the doors to the bedrooms had been left open. Iron framed beds with mildewed mattresses no one had slept on in years stood forlornly next to empty chests of drawers and chairs riddled with woodworm that no one would ever sit on. Green mould oozed along the edges of the window glass, fed by the constant trickle of condensation. Even placing each foot gently onto the bare floorboards didn't stop them creaking and I paused, holding my breath, expecting to be discovered, but the singing continued. I crept on. Grey cobwebs festooned the corners as spiders spun their lives away in the dust and silence. Mouse droppings and fallen plaster, dead wasps and moths littered the floor. I reached the last room, its door just ajar. With the lightest touch it swung back. The singer stood with her back to me looking out of the cracked window across the lawn towards the marsh. She was shorter than me with long dark hair, in a maid's dress just like my own. As I stepped tentatively forward the floorboards creaked loudly, giving me away. I stopped dead, waiting.

Slowly, slowly she turned around still singing, "Bye Zilla Bunting, the Marsh Ink's gone ahunting, gone to find another skin … to hide in …" Her hair lifted, floating as if the window were open and letting in the breeze, but it was shut and the cold air was still. "But it don't hide do it. It's there for everyone to see … till it don't want to be seen no more … then it moves … slides around inside you like worms in the dead." Her voice frayed into fine threads of whisper that floated like her hair, curling around the room, twisting around me as her grey eyes widened. I froze to the spot. I couldn't move a muscle as she drifted across the room towards me. Her pale face was solid, real, but the hand she reached out was translucent, misty. I held my breath. With icy fingers she delicately touched my cheek then her own. It was stained with a grey mark, much smaller than mine, the familiar stain of Marsh Ink. "It's the smell that gets you first … so warm … so kind … fills you up with summer." Outside a pigeon's wings clattered as it flew past the window. Frost crept slowly across the inside of the glass panes. She drew even closer. "Only had a little fall … I weren't bad enough to die … tricked I was." Only inches away from me she emanated coldness, freezing the air between us. From somewhere behind me I heard footsteps, heels clicking and a floorboard creaked. She scowled, hissing, "I weren't ready to go!"

Suddenly Mrs Pinkney's voice snapped, "What on earth are you doing up here?"

I gasped and in the blink of an eye the

girl was gone. My heart thumped, pounding so hard I could hear it. I sucked in a lungful of air, squawking with fright, "Didn't you see her?"

"Who?" a sneer started on Mrs Pinkney's top lip.

"A ghost. A ghost girl. She was standing right here. Right in front of me. Only a second ago."

"There's no one else here." Mrs Pinkney called back over her shoulder, "Did you hear that, Mrs Egmore? Zilla's talking to herself. It's the Marsh Ink. It's gone to her head." Mrs Egmore's toady face appeared in the doorway looking as if she had a bad smell under her nose. She snorted her disgust as Mrs Pinkney continued, "Keep on like this and it'll be the asylum for you, Zilla Bunting. Begging your pardon, Mrs Egmore, no offence intended."

Mrs Egmore sniffed, "None taken."

Mrs Pinkney's fingers dug into my arm, "Back downstairs with you!" I was propelled towards the door and along the landing. Not that I needed any encouragement. She released her grip at the top of the stairs and, only too eager to get away, I ran down them, making a dash for the kitchen. Heart still pounding I leant up against the wall and took huge gulps of air. My knees shook as I stood listening, waiting for them to follow me. Then I heard their voices in the corridor, the attic door slam, the steel bolt slide across and their footsteps dying away as they headed towards the hall.

"Zilla?" Miss Lamb walked in carrying a pile of freshly ironed sheets. "Is something wrong?"

"A ghost, Miss Lamb! I saw a ghost in the attic!"

"Deep breaths, Zilla, deep breaths." Miss Lamb carefully placed her sheets down on the table, and took my hand, "You're frozen! Come and sit by the range." I didn't want to sit down. I wanted to run. Run away, as far as I could, to anywhere that felt safe, anywhere away from Creakie Hall. I tried to protest but she wasn't taking 'No' for an answer so I made myself sit on the chair even though my feet were twitching. She looked at me thoughtfully, "Did anyone else see it?"

"No. But Mrs Pinkney and Mrs Egmore caught me up there. They think I'm going mad."

"No. They're just saying that. They know full well this house is haunted — and they know who by."

My jaw dropped. Wide eyed I asked,

"Who? Who is she?"

Miss Lamb listened for a moment for sounds from the corridor but heard none, "Good. Mrs Pinkney must still be with Mrs Egmore." Then she sat down beside me, "The ghost is that of poor Ada Goodwin. The other soul infected by the Marsh Ink. She came here from the orphanage. Such a good worker. I was very fond of her — a sweet girl."

"But what did she die of?"

"A fall. Down the attic stairs. Most tragic. She did not appear to be injured but very badly shaken so we sent her back to her bed. I sent up one of the other maids with a cup of tea and when I went to check on her an hour later her spirit had already departed. The doctor said it must have been an internal injury … perhaps her brain."

"But, Miss Lamb, she said she was tricked. She said she wasn't ready to go." My heart was calming down.

Miss Lamb shuddered, "Tricked? How strange. Poor, dear girl. She was far too young to die. It was awful … absolutely awful. I've often wondered — if I'd called the doctor sooner — if I'd done something — perhaps she would still be with us." She put her hand to her chest, lips pressed together for a moment, struggling to hold in her emotions.

I waited for a while before asking, “Is she always up there?”

“She’s appeared several times in different rooms but mostly the attic.”

“Is that why we all sleep down here?” I was sitting so close to the range that its warmth was bringing life back into my frozen fingers.

“Indeed it is. I should apologise for misleading you both when you arrived, it’s been preying on my conscience. And for telling you that the stairs were unusable. I suppose they are in a way but for a completely different reason. Although the attic is not unpleasant accommodation none of us could face going up there after Ada appeared. We never knew when she was going to show herself — the maids were absolutely terrified, poor girls. So we all decamped to this part of the house — it was a bit of a squeeze but it’s the only part that she’s never been seen in. The other staff left. Quite understandably. They couldn’t bear it any longer. I’ve considered it many times myself but at my time of life ….” Her words tailed away and for a minute we sat in silence before Miss Lamb cleared her throat, “Very few people want to work in a house as blighted as this one.” She ran her hand over the pile of sheets, "And you told Mrs Pinkney and Mrs Egmore what you'd seen?"

"They didn't believe me. Mrs Pinkney said I'd end up in an asylum. Then she said, 'Begging your pardon, no offence intended,' to Mrs Egmore." It suddenly struck me as odd.

Miss Lamb raised an eyebrow, "And what did Mrs Egmore reply?"

"'None taken.' She wasn't upset at all."

"So Mrs Pinkney knows about Mr Henry Egmore then. The family secret is out." Miss Lamb's eyes lit up, "So that's why Mrs Egmore won't get rid of her – she knows too much."

Chapter 12

A week after their confrontation Miss Lamb was still moaning about Mrs Bloggs every time she came back from the village, "I'll wipe the smirk off her face one day — you see if I don't!"

I was past caring. If the village didn't want me then I didn't want the village. I'd come up with a plan, a plan to get away. I was going to write to Mrs Sowter in Norwich and ask for my old job back, any job, anything at all, just as long as I got away from Creakie Hall with its endless dirt and its ghost. Every time I ventured away from the servants quarters my nerves were on edge, expecting to see Ada through every doorway or hear her strange, wistful singing. Whenever I was sweeping out some dusty corner, making up the fires in the gloom of the early mornings or felt a chilly draught in the hall the hair on the back of my neck would stand on end. With every unexpected creak or groan of the old house I'd jump like a nervous rabbit. I hated being alone in the empty old rooms and always tried to leave the doors open so I could run away if she appeared.

The household had its own lunchtime

routine. Mrs Egmore would take her afternoon nap and Mr Egmore and Arnold would take Tibbs along with them for their afternoon walk while I cleared away the crockery, the bread, the butter, the cheese and the jars of jam from the table. Miss Lamb would sit down with a cup of tea, perch her reading spectacles on her nose and read out all the interesting bits from the periodicals. That afternoon she started with the suffragette news, the latest prison hunger strike and the courageous actions of the five women who had chained themselves to the town hall railings. The advertisements were studied next, the latest bicycles, laundry soap and a tonic that would bring cheer to even the dreariest heart. I listened half-heartedly, my thoughts drifting to my plan of escape, to what I could say in my letter to Mrs Sowter, when there was a knock on the door and a small voice called, "Miss Lamb? Are you there?"

Miss Lamb beamed, "Come in, Lucy, come in!" Lucy. I hadn't spoken to her since that day, Marsh Ink day. She pushed the door open a crack and squeezed through as if she was trying to get in unnoticed. "Have you got it?" Miss Lamb asked eagerly.

Lucy nodded, "It's all right, Miss

Lamb, 'cos Mrs Bloggs is in bed with a bad cold and Mr Bloggs, he don't care what I do 'cos she's always bossing him about and now he's got to take charge he can do the bossing and he said to me, he said, 'You go out and have a bit of fun, girl, while the missus isn't looking.' So I come here but I can't stay too long 'cos I know she'll be looking out of the bedroom window. She's not so ill that she can't be nosy." Her words streamed out with barely a breath between them.

I looked at their happy faces, "Got what?"

"Grease paint," Lucy pulled a small pot out of her pocket.

"I was looking along the shelves at the grocers when I spotted it and it occurred to me that it may solve your problem," Miss Lamb took the small pot from Lucy. "If we can't get the Marsh Ink out then we may at least be able to disguise it."

"Mrs Bloggs got some in the shop to try it out on the customers but Miss Lamb didn't want to buy it there and then 'cos if it works and hides the ink then you can tell everybody that the ink run out of your nose again. And they don't ever need know that it's really the grease paint just hiding it. So Miss Lamb give me the money to pay for it and I had to sneak it out," Lucy beamed, delighted to get one over on Mrs Bloggs.

Neither Mrs Sowter nor Mum had approved of grease paint. They both said we should be happy with what nature has given us and not try to improve on it, because we'd only fail. But then neither of them had ever had to tackle this problem and I was ready to give anything a go. Miss Lamb handed me the pot and I read the label, "Madame Odette's Satin Beauty Cream. Imparts radiance and conceals all blemishes. Created by the world renowned House of Odette, Paris, London, New York. It sounds wonderful," I took the top off and sniffed, "smells nice too."

"It's very popular with the young ladies in London. Shall we give it a try?" Miss Lamb was itching to get her hands on the cream inside the pot and I nodded, half hopeful, half anticipating failure. She gently smeared some on my face and smoothed it with her fingers then stood back with Lucy to have a good look, both nodding approval, both smiling, "I think we have found a solution to your problem. Take a look in the mirror."

My insides rolled over as I walked into the corridor. The mirror by the coat pegs hung ready to pass judgement and, despite Lucy and Miss Lamb's enthusiasm, hope deserted me and I thought Mme Odette's Satin Beauty Cream would fail the test. But to my amazement the grey patch had almost disappeared. The grease paint wasn't quite the same colour as my skin but it was a huge improvement. "Will it all wear off?"

"I don't know," Lucy looked vague, "I've never worn any."

"I think it does eventually," Miss Lamb guessed, "but then you just have to apply more. Even if you don't use it every day you could apply it when you're leaving the house or going somewhere important."

I didn't have anywhere important to go but it seemed churlish to point it out. A twinge of guilt caught me unawares. They were doing their best to help me and I was doing my best to leave. "Is it very expensive?"

"Nothing for you to worry about. It will come out of the housekeeping. The Egmore's got you into this mess so if a few of their pennies help you out of it so much the better," Miss Lamb smiled. She was, on this occasion almost literally, the cat that got the cream.

Lucy shot a nervous look at the clock, "I've got to go. By the time I get back I'll have been gone nearly a whole hour and even if she is ill —"

"Absolutely," Miss Lamb nodded, "well done, Lucy, and thank you for your efforts. Zilla, why don't you walk back with Lucy, if only for a little way? Get some fresh air." We left her humming happily as she scoured the periodicals for more news of the suffragettes and we walked together to the end of the drive.

"I can't go any further — not to the village anyway."

Lucy shrugged, "Maybe one day soon. If you use the grease paint they'll get used to you again. After a bit they might forget about the Marsh Ink and everything'll go back to how it used to be."

I watched her scurrying along the road until she was almost out of sight. Clouds scudded across the blue sky, their shadows passing over the green scrub of the marsh, blown on by a cold, sharp wind. Hoping to get out of it in the shelter of the trees I headed towards the woodland. I felt light, a weight had lifted off my shoulders and the problem of the Marsh Ink could be easily overcome without resorting to drastic measures for its removal. My future suddenly looked brighter. Dried leaves skirled around my feet as I trod the path worn smooth by generations of feet, hopping over the roots that could have tripped me up, enjoying the sunshine that flooded through the canopy of bare branches above. I was stepping lively as the path dipped down, out of sight of the road, when I heard Tibbs barking. Between the ivy smothered tree trunks ahead I spotted Arnold walking beside Mr Egmore and, for the second time that day, my stomach rolled over. They were holding hands.

'Idiots! Bloody idiots!' Jaw stuck out, shoulders hunched, I yelled, "ARNOLD! ARNOLD!" Mr Egmore dropped Arnold's hand like a hot brick, striding away, and shouting for Tibbs to follow him.

Arnold's face screwed up as he stormed towards me, "What did you do that for?"

"IDIOT!" I screamed, "IDIOT! What do you think you're doing? You could get arrested." I whacked him again and again, "You could go to prison! You bloody, stupid idiot! Anyone could have seen you!" He raised his arms to protect himself from my blows, tried to take a step away from me but he wasn't fast enough and I whacked him again, "IDIOT! YOU STUPID, STUPID IDIOT!"

"STOP! STOP — stop hitting me," the colour drained from his face as the realisation of what could have happened sunk in, "Oh hell!" He slapped his forehead with the palm of his hand, "Didn't think. Just forgot — for a moment — I just forgot."

"Not good enough, Arnold, you can't forget. You mustn't forget — not ever — you know that. You know what'll happen if anyone sees you — you'll end up in prison — and not just you — him as well — both of you!"

He nodded miserably, "I know, I know. I'm sorry. It's just so quiet here. There's never anyone about."

"Yes there is. I saw Mrs Pinkney up here one time. You've got to be more careful. What if she sees you? What if she already has? Who's going to give you a job if you've been in prison? Idiot!"

"Alright, point taken. I'm sorry. We'll be more careful."

"You'd better be!"

"I will, Zilla, I will." He rubbed his arm and kept his distance in case I hit him again. We stood for a while under the bare branches of the trees, Arnold kicking at the dead leaves, me fuming, before he asked, "What are you doing here anyway? Run out of work?"

"No." Not even Arnold's stupidity was going to ruin my small triumph but I wasn't going to make it easy for him, "Can't you see anything different?"

It took him a moment to cotton on. Then he peered at my face, "Very impressive. You'd hardly know the Ink was there at all. Whose idea was this?"

"Miss Lamb. She saw it in the shop and Lucy brought it round for me to try."

"She's a good egg, Miss Lamb — and little Lucy."

I nodded but guilt was nipping at my insides again, "I know. But I want to leave. Arnold, it's horrible here now — with the village and Ada's ghost and everything."

"How many more times — there are no such things as ghosts! You'd had a very distressing experience with the Marsh Ink. You were just overwrought. You tell me that I'm an idiot and then you talk about seeing ghosts —"

"No, Arnold, I did see her — and it was awful — and I dread seeing her again — and I want to leave!"

Arnold groaned, "For the last time, Zilla, there are no such thing as ghosts. If you start talking to anyone else like this they'll think you're going mad — they'll think that the Ink has gone to your head." He was never going to believe me, never going to believe in ghosts. He turned away and started walking along the path. The cold wind bit into the gap between my scarf and the collar of my coat as I fell into step behind him and we made our way slowly back towards the road. "I'm going to write to Mrs Sowter to see if I can have my old job back. I can hide the Ink now so I don't have to tell her about it. Do you think they'll take me back?" Arnold didn't answer, just kept walking, picking his way over the tree roots. "Arnold, didn't you hear me? I said I'm going to write to Mrs —"

He snapped at me, "I heard you. But you can't write to her."

"Course I can. I know she'll help me if she can. She always said —"

"NO! You can't write to her, Zilla. She won't have you back. She can't."

Stunned, I stopped dead in my tracks. The wind and the leaves blew around me, moving endlessly. "What do you mean she won't have me back?"

He stopped walking and stood for a moment with his back to me, before turning slowly, sighing, "They won't have you back. I should've told you sooner but I didn't want to. I thought if you were happy here it wouldn't matter. The master found out about me … that's why we had to leave. They gave me enough time to find another post —"

"HE FOUND OUT? He could have put you in prison."

"He could have." Arnold's face was pale, pinched with cold, "Didn't want the scandal. Said he didn't want the family's good name dragged through the mud."

My mind reeled, as much as I felt angry that Arnold had been rejected I didn't see why I should be rejected as well, "But that's you … not me. Why won't they have me back?"

"He said if I was like it you might be too. It might be a family weakness. Inherited — in the blood. You're tainted by association. He didn't want me in his house and he didn't want you either." He looked at the ground, kicked at some leaves, "Sorry. I should've told you."

From the way his eyes avoided mine I knew it wasn't the whole story, "How long did they know about you?"

He kept his head down, "Not long. About a week before I told you we were leaving."

"And you found us these new jobs in a week?" My fists clenched, "How did you manage that?"

"I … um … I'd already met Charles — I mean Mr Egmore — in London."

"You already knew him! How long has

that been going on?"

"Since last summer." He still couldn't look at me.

"You lied to me. You rat! You set this up didn't you!" Anger made my face burn, no amount of grease paint could hide it.

Arnold looked up, spread his arms, imploring, "Don't be angry, Zilla, it was a chance for us to be together. And be safe. I wrote to him when I got the sack. He suggested it. We're happy. I never thought I'd get the chance to, you know — live with another man — a man I loved — and I do love him, Zilla, I really do."

My dream of escape collapsed in a heap, all my hopes in tatters, all thoughts of a return to the old house, to Mrs Sowter and my friends, in shreds and I wanted to thump him, put my hands around his throat and throttle him for deceiving me but Mum's words came into my head, 'Your brother is just as good as any other man. He should be able to love where he chooses but he can't so don't you begrudge it to him if he gets the chance.' It wasn't his love that I begrudged it was that he hadn't told me. Still smouldering with anger I said, "Well, you won't be safe if the two of you are caught holding hands. Arnold, you really are the limit. You should've told me!"

He shrugged, “I know,” and added feebly, “sorry.”

I whacked his arm again just for good measure and had the last word as I pushed past him, “You must be more careful. IDIOT!”

Chapter 13

Another Monday, another washday. I'd lit the fire under the copper early in the morning and by nine o'clock steam filled the laundry room. Sleeves rolled up, Mrs Pinkney rubbed and tubbed at the sink and wash-board, the clean smell of soap flakes filling the corridor and kitchen. Mr Egmore had a cold and a pile of well used handkerchiefs needed to be washed but Miss Lamb insisted that it was unpleasant and unhygienic for them to be washed with everything else. I agreed with her as I picked up the tongs and squashed them all into a large saucepan, filled it with water, added some soap flakes and left it all to boil on top of the range.

"Zilla," Miss Lamb called, "take this tea to Will. He's over by the lean-to." She thrust a cup filled with tea so stewed it was almost black into my hands and bustled back into the kitchen. I nipped into the scullery and grabbed a wrinkly, old apple from the pile on the windowsill. The back door swung shut behind me and I took a deep breath. Days like that were few and far between that winter. The sun shone brilliantly and the air was crystal clear, the kind of day to blow away all the cobwebs.

Sparrows pecking for seeds in the clumps of weeds growing around the yard scattered and the wind blew my skirt against my legs as I crossed the backyard to the stable block. Five stables, all standing empty, the disused tack room and the huge doors of the old coach house, all had to be passed before I reached the lean-to where the logs were stacked. I hated walking there in the evenings imagining all manner of horrors that lurked in the damp shadows so I always made sure the log baskets were full before it got dark. But nothing could hide on a day that bright. Duke tossed his black head, restless between the cart shafts, the sound of his horseshoes ringing against the flints in the yard floor as he stamped his hooves and waited for Will to finish offloading more logs.

"Tea, Will," I shouted as I got closer.

He tossed the logs he was holding onto the top of the stack, "Good on you, Zilla, I'm gasping." I held up the apple and he grinned, "Go on then, just keep your fingers straight or he'll give them a nibble." He gave Duke's side a rub, "Give him an apple or a mint and he'll love you for ever." It was reassuring to know that somebody would even if he was a horse.

Duke's big, soft lips nuzzled into my

hand and the apple disappeared to the sound of contented munching. “Let’s have a look then,” Will stared long and hard straight at my face, at its grey, Marsh Ink stain and pronounced, “Well it’s not good, Zilla, but I can hardly talk.” He laughed, “We make a right pair, the two of us. Dad says we could do for a pair of bookends!”

In the sparkling sunshine his birthmark looked an even deeper red than usual, like someone had poured port wine on his face. For the first time I felt brave enough to look at it directly and ask him the question that had been troubling me since Marsh Ink day, the day I was infected, “Do you mind … I mean … do you mind having a mark?”

He looked up at the sky for a moment, thinking, “Well, I’ve never been without it … don’t even think of it most of the time … but now and then I get a bit irritated … not really with my mark … but I get a bit riled with other people … when some stupid git starts staring.” His head tipped slightly to left and then slightly to the right as he weighed up the pros and cons, “But if I was in your position I’d mind. Being infected like … that’s a bit different. And you being a girl and all — being pretty matters to girls. It don’t matter so much to boys — we can get away with being a bit odd looking … even downright ugly, but it's harder on girls."

I rubbed Duke's neck, "They won't let me in the village now — Mrs Bloggs and the rest of them."

"We all heard about the showdown. Can't imagine Miss Lamb took that well. Old Bag Bloggs — that's what Dad calls her — she's a bossy old cow right enough but give the rest of them time. I reckon in six months when none of them or their children have got infected they'll all come round, you'll see. It'll all blow over." Duke tossed his head and Will drank his tea and I lingered just to have their company for a few minutes and to feel the sun on my face. I wanted to ask if he believed in ghosts, if he'd ever seen anything strange at the house or the woods or the marsh but the sunshine was so bright and the day so cheerful that it was the wrong thing to talk about and I couldn't find the right words.

"Zilla!" Mrs Pinkney interrupted our moment of happiness. She walked halfway across the yard and plonked down a full basket of laundry, "Stop standing about. We can't waste a good drying day. Peg this out!" I groaned, not wanting to drag myself back to the endless grind of Creakie Hall.

"No rest for the wicked," Will laughed,

"best get to it before Mrs P gets riled." I left him leaning up against the cart finishing his tea.

Picking up the basket I headed for the washing lines strung out across the yard. One line was already full of white sheets in full sail, billowing in the wind. I held the pillowcases up to the next line, pushing the pegs over the wet fabric to hold them fast. That line full I had to start on the third one. To reach it I pushed the pillowcases out of the way. As they parted she was right there in front of me, in broad daylight, the ghost of Ada Goodwin, her face as white as the laundry, eyes blazing, "I weren't ready to go!" The wind stopped blowing. "I weren't ready to go." The birds were silent. "I weren't ready to go." I gripped the pillowcases tighter. "I weren't ready to go!" I could hear my own heart pounding as she drew slowly closer. She lifted her misty hand to touch the grey stain on her cheek. "Never did me no harm … it ain't pretty but it never did me no harm." The pillowcases grew colder, their wet fibres freezing together, freezing onto my locked fingers. Unable to let go, unable to run, I was rooted to the spot. I listened to her icy whispers as they twisted through the sunlight, meshing around me, "It'll come for you …

one day soon … it'll come for you."

My lips chilled, a tiny mist of breath left my mouth, "What will?"

"The beast … it'll come for you … like it came for me … like it came for Tommy … it'll sniff you out." Her translucent hands reached out towards me. Her dead cold fingers caressed my stained cheek. "It's so cruel … so cold … no heart inside … it don't care." I heard the clip of heels crossing the backyard and she must have heard them too, leaning forward until she was so close her frozen face almost touched mine. A frayed whisper full of fear left her pale lips, "Don't you stay here no more."

"What are you up to? Seeing ghosts again?" Mrs Pinkney's voice snapped me back to the laundry and Ada snapped away. I was left facing nothing but the empty yard and the empty washing line and the empty blue sky.

My hands still gripped the frozen pillowcases, knuckles white, but I forced out, "No, Mrs Pinkney, no ghosts."

"That's just as well," her warm breath tickled the back of my neck as she stood behind me, "there's always a place in the mad house for sad little girls like you." She nudged me in my ribs, "Get a move on then. Like I told you we can't waste a good drying day. Laundry won't dry in the basket, will it!" I heard her heels clicking away, back towards the house, but it was another minute before I could release my fingers from the pillowcases. The bright winter sun dazzled my eyes and the sheets billowed cleanly but the wind carried something else with it, Ada's distant voice singing, her words like fine threads blown across the yard, "Bye Zilla Bunting, the beast has come ahunting, come to get what's in your skin …."

Chapter 14

"Zilla! Come quick!" Miss Lamb hollered along the corridor. I threw down my scrubbing brush, jumped to my feet and ran to the front door to join her. A car with deepest, glossy green paintwork, brass trims shining, gleaming with newness, was creeping along the driveway with Mr Egmore at the wheel. Arnold sat beside him, beaming. Tibbs raced across the lawn and gave chase, tail wagging frantically, barking all the way.

"I didn't know he could drive." I watched as it bounced a couple of times over the ruts.

Miss Lamb threw her hands in the air with delight. "Oh yes. He learnt last summer. Isn't it thrilling? Are you ready?"

"Ready for what?"

"Mr Egmore has promised to take us out. He's going to convey us along the coast road in his motorcar. Its top speed is forty miles per hour. I'm sure I'll get dizzy."

I was already dizzy. The twentieth century had reached Creakie Hall on four wheels and the excitement went straight to my head as I raced down the corridor, grabbed our coats, running back full tilt just as the car came to a stop by the front door, its thin wheels spraying water from the puddles left by the overnight rain.

"What do you think then? Isn't it a beauty?" Arnold hopped out as if he had been in and out of cars all his life. I ran my hand lightly over the smooth bonnet, the metal almost buzzing with the electrifying thrill of the new age and holding the prospect of future travels to exhilarating places, of wonderful escape. I peered in through the windows. Unable to resist the temptation I pressed down the brass door handle and very, very carefully opened the door. Inside the leather seats were padded and buttoned, the height of luxury, no expense had been spared. "Mr Egmore's going to use the old coach house as a garage. Then we can keep it clean and the brass work polished — protect it from the weather."

Eager to get started Miss Lamb pulled on her coat and cleared her throat rather loudly.

Mr Egmore chuckled, "Point taken, Miss Lamb. Well, ladies, are you ready to join the modern age? To experience the heady delights of the motorcar? To feel the power of the internal combustion engine?"

"Absolutely," Miss Lamb trilled.

'Just let me at it,' I thought, 'anything

that gets me away from here.' Out loud I said politely, "Yes, please!"

But Miss Lamb had barely got her foot on the running board when Mrs Egmore ruined the moment, snapping, "Charles! I think you forget yourself!"

He groaned, loudly enough for her to hear but she took no notice, "Of course, Mother, my apologies. Perhaps Miss Lamb could accompany you and," he nodded to me, "Zilla can wait her turn."

"I think not. Miss Lamb can wait. I prefer to be accompanied by Mrs Pinkney." They stood in the doorway, Mrs Egmore with the furry skin of some poor, dead creature wrapped around her shoulders, chin up, glaring down her nose and Mrs Pinkney with a smug smile on her face, playing the part of the dutiful servant for all it was worth.

Miss Lamb's face turned pink. For a moment her foot seemed glued to the running board. As the promise of excitement, of joining the modern world, died her face twitched. She straightened her back, put her foot back on the ground and moved stiffly away. A terse "Of course, ma'am," forced out from between her lips.

We dutifully stood side by side in the cold as drops of rain spat from the grey clouds onto the immaculate car windows. Arnold and Mr Egmore admired the paint work and discussed the engine and Tibbs sniffed at the wheels. We all waited for Mrs Pinkney to help Mrs Egmore put her hat and coat and gloves on and I wished with every fibre of my being that the rotten car would end up in a ditch with Mrs Pinkney and Mrs Egmore both dead. But then I thought of Arnold and felt slightly guilty. I didn't want him dead.

Arnold waited by the door for Mrs Egmore to take her seat. She smiled her toady smile and said acidly, "Real ladies first, Miss Lamb." And then they drove away, Arnold still beaming and Mrs Pinkney smirking from the back seat.

"After all the years I've worked here, all the devotion, all the loyalty — and that bloody bitch goes first! This really is beyond the limit!" I'd never heard Miss Lamb swear before. I was shocked. She stormed off, doors slamming behind her, leaving Tibbs and me alone in the hall. The moment was over, all the pleasure sucked out of the day. I plonked myself down on the stairs, gazing out of the windows as rain trickled down the glass panes. Thirty minutes passed and the rain had given way to general gloom when the blonde haired boy appeared, the boy I'd seen on the marsh. Small and distant, he stood by the hedge on the other side of the wide lawn watching the house, hardly moving, as if he was waiting for someone. I walked over to the windows for a better look and he waved frantically, wanting my attention. He had it. No one new ever came to Creakie Hall and no one ever waved.

"Miss Lamb, can I go out for a bit? "I yelled along the corridor.

The answer came back, "Do what you like — take as long as you like! Why should I care?"

Tibbs was yapping at my heels and I buttoned up my coat as I hurried along the driveway. When I reached the road I could see the boy's head bobbing along the path across the marsh and I followed, trying not to fall as I skidded my way between the puddles, Tibbs splashing straight through them. He led us far out onto the marsh, between the creeks and the gullies, between the green scrub and the tall, fluffy headed reeds and then vanished. I looked around for any sign of him but there was none. I should have felt annoyed at being led on a wild goose chase but I didn't. As I wandered along the freedom of the wide open space lifted my spirits. The sun peeped through breaks in the cloud sending down shafts of light and I turned my face up to catch the rays, "Blow Creakie Hall. Blow the car. Let Mrs Pinkney and Mrs Egmore have their ride. There'll be other times. One day I'll be gone from here. One day I'll be free of them forever." My thoughts turned to Ada. I hadn't seen her again and although her last words, 'The beast has come ahunting, come to get what's in your skin,' had terrified me at the time I had begun to think they were only silly words, only said to scare me. I had been a bag of nerves, jumping at every unexpected sound, looking over my shoulder, around corners, scanning every hedge and tree trunk, even under the bed, for the beast but there had been no sign of it and I had grown sick and tired of being on edge all the time. The beast, I decided, was no more than a nasty joke. Even my fear, it seemed, had its limits and my thoughts turned back to the blonde haired boy. He was a mystery and I badly wanted to find him.

"Where's he gone, Tibbs?" I patted the top of his head but he just whimpered. "You're a dog, can't you find him? Can't you follow his scent?" I didn't expect to get an answer back but he yowled and backed off and then started growling, "What's wrong?"

The reeds ahead of us began to move,

swaying gently in the wrong direction, against the breeze. Then I heard the boy singing, "Bye Zilla Bunting, the beast has come —" The hair on the back of my neck stood up. Tibbs took off, racing away, barking frantically. Panic hit me. I didn't wait to hear the rest. I spun round to chase after Tibbs, back to Creakie Hall, back to safety, but my boots slipped in the mud. Face down in the mud and water, trembling, every nerve on edge I heard his voice coming closer and closer, "Bye Zilla Bunting, the beast has come ahunting, across the marsh and up the wood, to find Zilla Bunting." The mud around my fingers began to freeze, turning white, crackling. Icy water dripped onto the back of my neck, trickling around my throat in a frozen necklace. "I know it don't rhyme but I'm no good at rhymes … not like Ada … she's good at rhymes." I lifted my head to see his ghostly, bare feet, misty as sea fog, standing next to me. Slowly, slowly, breath in gasps, every nerve quivering, I forced myself to roll over and face him. In short trousers and with no boots he was dressed for summer. He leaned over me, no more than eight years old, so innocent and eager with deathly pale eyes that stared straight into mine and on his wan face the familiar grey stain of Marsh Ink. It was Tommy, Tommy Cottle, the dead boy. "What you scared of?" His voice was eerily thin, like fine gossamer cobwebs drifting on a breeze.

"Nothing," my words barely made it out of my mouth, "nothing."

He wiped the back of his hand across his nose, "Guess what we done?" I shook my head and he giggled, "We done the same thing — we got Ink up our noses!" His hands, that had seemed so solid when he waved, were as faded as his feet. With an icy, transparent finger he touched the ink stain on my face, "Ada says you snuffed it all up … the whole book … I only done three pages! … And Ada only done two … but you done all of it. "

Instinctively I squirmed backwards along the path, shuddering as I struggled to my feet, "What do you want from me?"

"We want you to go away … over the hills and far, far away or the beast'll come back … that's what Ada says. It's sniffing for you — we can feel it sniffing, me and Ada." He took a step towards me and I realised he was wet. Water dripped from his hair and face, rivulets running over his shoulders and grubby shirt. Drips fell from the frayed bottom of his trousers but never reached the ground.

Horror gnawed at my insides. My skin began to crawl. I whispered "You're wet … Why? … Why are you wet?" A curlew's burbling song, lonely, haunting, carried across the emptiness of the marsh.

His listened, smiling for a moment. Like a dandelion clock caught by a breeze, his words scattered, their sound so thin I could barely hear him, "Ink likes it here … don't it." And he was gone.

I stood there, shaking, covered in mud, trying to pull myself together when a soft sensation spread from my face, warming my blood in its veins, filling me up with summer. He was right. The Marsh Ink did like it there.

Chapter 15

"Miss Lamb, can you do me a favour, please?" There was only two weeks until Christmas. She looked up from the newspaper, the suffragettes had thrown a brick through a window at the town hall and she was with them in spirit if not in body. "I want to get Arnold a Christmas present but there's nowhere I can go to buy one." She nodded, mouth still full of toast. "Could you buy him two pairs of good quality, woollen socks, for me please? Black. I've got the money here," I pulled it out of my apron pocket. "His socks are disgusting. There's more holes than sock and I can't bear to darn them anymore."

She swallowed her toast and held out her hand to take the money, "Of course. I just wish you were coming with us to London. A trip away would do you the world of good. You could have worn the grease paint."

London, even the name was exciting. The crowds, the grand shops with their Christmas decorations and even grander ladies in their flamboyant hats, the Tower of London, the Houses of Parliament and Buckingham Palace, how I ached to see it all.

I longed to sit in the circle at the Music Hall and watch Vesta Tilley and Little Titch, longed to listen to Marie Lloyd and watch a performance of Peter Pan. Mr Egmore would drive them to the railway station and they would take the train to Liverpool Street. But Mrs Egmore could not be left alone and Mrs Pinkney was visiting her sister so I was lumbered. Miss Lamb was due back the following day but Arnold and Mr Egmore would stay in London until the day after. The sun was barely up the next day when I waved them goodbye from the front step, Tibbs sitting by my feet wagging his tail cheerfully. It was a half cloud, half sun day, a good day to travel, but a bad one to be stuck indoors dusting and waiting hand and foot on her Imperial Majesty, Mrs Egmore.

"Zilla," somehow her voice managed to carry to wherever I was working, "make me some fresh tea." "Zilla, find my embroidery." "Zilla, go to my room and fetch my book," her demands were endless. At ten o'clock I was half-heartedly flicking a duster over the mahogany sideboard in the hall when the front door opened and there stood Mrs Pinkney. So much for visiting her sister.

"I didn't think you were coming today," I twisted the duster through my fingers, "Miss

Lamb said you'd gone to see your sister."

She sneered at me, "Changed my mind, didn't I. Not that it's any of your business — or Miss Lamb's." She slipped her scarf off and tossed it down onto a chair, "Keep working, girl, it's what you're paid for."

As I ran the duster over the top of the sideboard the shine came back to the wood and the inlaid pattern of shells and ribbons sung again. But as fast as I got rid of dust in Creakie Hall more would fall from the old plaster ceilings, hanging in the air, catching the light, ready to settle down on the furniture. All the time I worked I could hear them talking and laughing. Curiosity got the better of me so I sneaked over to the drawing room door, still just ajar, and peeked through the crack just in time to see Mrs Pinkney pull a full bottle of gin from the pocket of her coat, take out the stopper and hand it to Mrs Egmore. Mrs Egmore handed her back an empty bottle which she slipped into her coat pocket and then Mrs Egmore poured a good slug of gin into her teacup from her new bottle. Tibbs gave me away, opening the door wide as he pushed past my legs and padded into the room. They both looked up. "What do you think you're looking at?" snapped Mrs Pinkney, sharp as a needle.

I shook my head, "Nothing."

"Better be nothing. You didn't see nothing and you didn't hear nothing," her pretty face was distorted by spite. "One word from you to anyone and you'll be out on the street."

Mrs Egmore laughed, "Our little secret, Zilla, if you don't want to end up in the workhouse." She raised her teacup as if she was toasting me, "Chin, chin," and downed her gin laced tea in one go. "Zilla, get that revolting dog out of here. It stinks."

Tibbs didn't care for their company and came as soon as I called him. Mrs Pinkney almost caught his tail in the door as she slammed it behind him. I hurried away, certain that Miss Lamb wouldn't mind if her instructions to give the hall a thorough clean before she came back were left unfulfilled, and beat the retreat to the kitchen, to the warmth of the range and the singing of the kettle. I couldn't stop my heart from beating too fast and the lump in my throat stuck there. "Arnold would never see me on the street or in the workhouse. Never!" I said to myself and I knew it was true but since Mum had gone the fear of being penniless and homeless often came to haunt me. I wished Arnold was with me. Not swanning around London with

Mr Egmore. Tibbs stretched himself out in his favourite spot and I started washing up the breakfast things, taking small comfort where I could find it, soaking my hands in the warm water and taking deep, steamy breaths. I was wiping the dish cloth over a pretty blue and white china cup when I caught the sound of Mrs Pinkney's heels clipping on the corridor tiles. She was coming to find me and there was nowhere I could hide, nowhere I could run to.

She stormed through the door and didn't mince her words, "Keep your mouth shut — d'you hear me?"

I tried to be brave, stand up for myself like Mum always said I should, "Mr Egmore says there's to be no alcohol in the house."

"I don't give a damn what Mr Egmore says," she marched straight across the kitchen and grabbed hold of my wrist, her finger nails digging in, "and as for Mrs Egmore, if she wants to drink herself to death I'm not about to stop her. I'll help her on her way. She asks for gin so I bring it — I'm a good servant — I do what I'm told." Her nostrils flared as she scowled, "Them and their bloody book. They should suffer for what they done to Tommy and Ada. They'd still be here if it weren't for that book. One way or another they should pay."

"What about me?" I wrenched my hand away from her, "I've been infected too and it wasn't my fault."

Surprised to hear me answer back, she raised her eyebrows and let go of my wrist, "True, I suppose. I told all the others to get out and they did. They weren't stupid. They did what they were told. And that's my advice to you and your brother. Leave before it's too late. Before you end up like Tommy and Ada. And don't you go forgetting, you still owe me a favour — I never told anyone when I found you in the woods with Ezra."

I rubbed my wrist, "I know. But if I don't tell anyone about this we'll be even, won't we?" Tibbs whined and tried to hide under the kitchen table.

She glared at me then nodded, "Alright then, we're even. But not a word, d'you understand, not a single word to Mr Egmore or I'll be after you." I nodded and she turned away, heels clicking on the kitchen tiles, "Don't you get in my way, Zilla Bunting!" The hall door slammed behind her. Help was far away, speeding along the railway tracks to London and I was alone. I couldn't hold the tears in any longer.

Chapter 16

I stayed in the kitchen with Tibbs, not wanting to leave, for fear of what I might find beyond the hall door, ghost or beast or Mrs Pinkney. At quarter past eleven she shouted along the corridor that she was leaving. The bell didn't ring for the rest of the morning but at one o'clock anxiety got the better of me and I steeled my nerves to see if Mrs Egmore had actually drunk herself to death. Not wanting to find her dead on my own I called Tibbs to come with me. I knew he would be useless but any support was better than none. He padded along, woofing softly every now and then. Silence filled the hall but nothing was lurking in the shadows, no ghosts or beasts. I crept past the furniture, still covered by a fine layer of dust, past my discarded duster, and stopped at the drawing room door, listening for signs of life. Hearing the low rumbling of Mrs Egmore's snores I gently pushed the door back and there she was, spark out, flat on the sofa, but at least she was only dead drunk and not completely dead. My feet made no sound as I tiptoed across the carpet and, as quietly as I could, made up the fire. Her teacup and saucer had rolled away under the side table. I had to kneel down to reach them and Tibbs took advantage, thinking I was about to start playing he bounced over to me and licked my face.

"Get off, Tibbs, you mucky pup," I said softly, thinking my voice might wake Mrs Egmore, but he didn't stop. With one hand holding the saucer and the other searching under the table for the cup it was impossible to push him away and he had another lick. The Marsh Ink in my face began to move, squirming like a giggly child, tickling my face from the inside. The sensation was so funny I burst out laughing, quickly clapping my hand over my mouth to keep the sound in. I looked at Mrs Egmore, in case I'd woken her, but her snores rumbled on. Balancing the cup on the saucer I ruffled the fluff on Tibbs' head, "You daft old boy!" He growled, showed the whites of his eyes and snarled. "Tibbs! What's wrong?" His tail between his legs he raced for the door.

I got to my feet, looking around the room to see what had upset him but saw nothing strange until my eyes reached the window. "Bye Zilla Bunting, the beast has come ahunting, come to get what's in your skin." The cup and saucer fell from my fingers, rolling away across the carpet. My breath caught in my throat. My heart stood still. Outside the window, white faced, Ada and Tommy stood side-by-side looking in. The three of us stared at each other, all our faces stained by the Marsh Ink, all linked together in that strange way. Frost formed around the edges of the window, creeping silently across the panes. The room chilled. My skin prickled with goosebumps. Fear, like needles, ran up my spine. Smiling, Tommy raised a small, misty hand and waved.

"Zilla, you got to listen to us," Ada's voice whispered through the frozen glass, "it's coming to get you. It's sniffing you out. You got to run."

"Run away … Zilla … run away," the smile fell from Tommy's face, water trickled from his wet hair. They looked so young, so fragile, that my heart went out to them and my fear left me, in its place only a terrible, aching sadness.

"Zilla," Mrs Egmore grumbled, half asleep. Startled, my eyes left the window for a split second to look at her but when I looked back Ada and Tommy were gone. "Zilla, fetch my wrap."

"Yes, ma'am," I mumbled, gazing at the empty window. She groaned again and in the next moment resumed her snoring, the rumbles gently filling the room.

I took a step forward, expecting them to reappear but hoping they wouldn't, then another but the window remained empty. I felt sick, "Don't come back again, please don't. Not today. Not without Arnold and Miss Lamb," I pleaded over and over as I bent to pick up the cup and saucer. "Not today, not today." The cup rattled on its porcelain saucer as my hands trembled. I didn't want to leave the drawing room. Mrs Egmore's lively, if drunken, snores were easier to cope with than the dead eyes of Tommy and Ada. But I knew I couldn't stay in the drawing room all day and after half an hour I made a dash for the kitchen.

I stayed there for the rest of the afternoon, trying not to look at the windows in case a ghostly face was looking back at me. Outside the gloom of the day gave way to twilight and by four o'clock the darkness I had been dreading enveloped us. The longer I was in the house by myself the larger it seemed, the rooms silent and forbidding, abandoned by everyone except the spiders spinning their webs in the corners that the feather duster couldn't reach. The creaks and groans were so loud in the emptiness it was as if the house was bemoaning its fate. I lit all the oil lamps and candles and banked up the range, hoping desperately that the light and the heat might drive Ada and Tommy away. Potatoes peeled, carrot sliced and the remains of the previous days beef pie ready I braced myself to see if Mrs Egmore would even be capable of eating. Tibbs didn't want to be alone either and we stuck together like glue as we ventured along the corridor and across the hall. The oil lamps guttered and the doors towered over me as I looked left and right into every shadowy nook and dark cranny for ghosts or beast or both. Taking a deep breath I pushed open the drawing room door to find Mrs Egmore sitting, almost upright, in her usual chair. "Zilla, I wish to take the air."

"Yes, ma'am," I shot across the room as she wobbled to her feet, grabbed my arm, and together we staggered out towards the front door. I opened it with one hand while trying to hold her up with the other and, dreading what might be outside, we crossed the threshold.

Thick mist floated over the far hedge, drifting around the black branches of the wind-blasted trees as Mrs Egmore tottered for several paces along the drive, managing to steady herself on the edge of the lawn. After a deep breath she muttered, "If I could leave here I would. This really is the most … godforsaken … vile… house … that … that …. ” She was unable to finish the sentence as her stomach began to heave. The gin made its comeback and she retched, mostly over the grass but some of it down her dress. Still trying to support her heavy body but trying not to breathe, I turned my face away to avoid the smell. At least it was outside and I wouldn't have to clean it up.

"Let's get you back indoors, ma'am," I tried to steer her back towards the front door. "Back in the warm. You'll catch your death out here."

"Death would be a blessed relief," she teetered in the doorway, "never, never … never … marry an idiot for money." Arnold was unlikely to force me into an unsuitable marriage in exchange for payment of his debts in the same way that Mrs Egmore's family had done to her so it was not a difficulty I was ever likely to face. I closed the front door firmly behind us, partly to keep her in but mostly to keep Ada, Tommy and the beast out.

"How about going to your bed for a proper sleep?" I suggested, hoping she would stay there until the next morning.

"Why not? A miserable bedroom is as

good as a miserable drawing room." With every step I grew more terrified that she would fall backwards down the stairs so I kept one hand on her back, propelling her forward. We made it to the landing, swayed our way into her bedroom and she collapsed on the bed. Pulling off her shoes and unbuttoning her dress I made encouraging sounds, "Nearly done, ma'am," while she moaned, "Godforsaken … hideous … idiot." If I ever needed proof of how difficult it is to undress somebody who is half asleep and dead drunk I had it that night but after fifteen minutes of monumental effort I had managed to remove her dress. I gave up on the idea of taking her corset off, pulled back the bed covers and half coaxed, half pushed her between the sheets. She went back to snoring. Exhausted, I flopped down on to the bedroom chair, head in my hands, "Oh Arnold, Oh Miss Lamb, I wish you were here."

Clinging to the hope that I wouldn't have to see her again until the morning I trailed back along the landing, her vomit stained dress folded up in my hands, but when I reached the top of the stairs I froze. The front door was ajar. A cold draught whispered through the house. Trying to stay out of sight, I peered over the banister rail and froze.

Below me, a dark, formless figure, was moving slowly through the shadows cast by the flickering oil lamp. Had the beast come for me? Had it waited until Arnold and Miss Lamb and Mr Egmore were away? It stopped, waiting, head on one side, listening. I held my breath, unable to move. It turned its head from left to right and sniffed. Was it trying to sniff me out, to catch the scent of my blood? Quiet as a wild cat on the prowl it reached out and turned the door handle to Mr Egmore's study, disappearing inside only to reappear moments later. My fingers stayed welded to the banister rail and my feet to the floor and I watched with horror as it crept in and out of the library. And it sniffed. But in a flicker of the light I caught the outline of a hat, a black coat, moving again, as a gloved hand reached out for the door handle of Mrs Egmore's writing room.

"Zilla?" A distant shout came from the servants' corridor, "Zilla? You here?"

Will. Will was in the house. I was no longer alone. With a sudden, mad rush of bravery and relief I shouted, "Here, Will, in the hall!" The figure below me moved smartly to the front door. Its face turned up towards me and Mrs Bloggs' heavy features appeared from under her hat.

"Oh there you are, Zilla. I called but nobody came," she said, all feigned innocence. "I've been stood here for the last ten minutes."

"I've been busy. Mrs Egmore is feeling poorly," there weren't enough stairs between the two of us for my liking but I felt compelled to walk down them, to show her I wasn't afraid, even though I was.

The servants' door into the hall opened and Will appeared just as I reached the last step. "Evening, Zilla … Mrs Bloggs. Miss Lamb asked me to drop-in and see that you were all right, make sure everything was ship-shape. Said you'd be on your own but it looks like she got that wrong."

"Don't mind me." Mrs Bloggs held out a small package, "Mr Egmore wanted me to deliver this while Miss Lamb was away. Walked all this way and me still with this cold." She sniffed, pulled a white handkerchief from her pocket and dabbed at her nose, "Expect it's her Christmas present." She eyed me up and down, "Young girl like you shouldn't be on her own with a man in the house. Mrs Egmore wouldn't want you having followers. That's taking advantage that is. People'll gossip. You'll get name for yourself."

"Now, Mrs Bloggs, that's enough of that sort of talk," Will said firmly.

"Only sayin'."

"Well don't say — or if you do say you ought to say something nice," a grin spread across his face and he added with a wink, "I don't want my reputation ruined."

She was not amused, sniffed and dabbed at her nose again, tweaked at her shapeless, heavy, black coat and waited for me to open the front door properly. She thrust the package into my hands and flounced out.

"Good night, Mrs Bloggs," I called at her back as she disappeared into the darkness. I got no answer.

"You all right?" Will's forehead wrinkled.

"I didn't know she was here. I didn't hear her knock or call."

"That don't surprise me. She can be a bit of a monster when she's a mind too." He followed me back through the servants' door, "You have to keep an eye on her or she'll be sticking her nose in where it's not wanted."

Just the sound of another voice in the house, another body moving, made everything better. The rooms shrunk back to their usual size and no beasts lurked in the corners. I offered Will a cup of tea and he accepted. We sat either side of the kitchen stove chatting about nothing in particular, the weather, Duke, Christmas, until it was time for him to leave. As I stood by the back door watching him walk away through the mist, I looked for any sign of Tommy and Ada, but there was none so I locked the door and went back to the warmth of the kitchen. The hours dragged on. At nine o'clock, with Tibbs' company, I checked on Mrs Egmore and found her still snoring soundly. I left the oil lamps alight on the landing and in the hall in case she called me in the night, at least that would have been my excuse if anyone had found them still burning but truth be told I couldn't face walking through the house in the dark with only a candle to guide the way. The shadows loomed too large. Half an hour later I climbed into my own bed. Tibbs lay in front of the fire. I had to spend the night in a haunted house but I wasn't going to do it alone. The covers pulled up tight under my chin I closed my eyes but I couldn't close my ears. Night sounds rustled and cracked twice as loudly as any noise in the day. The scratchings of mice behind the skirting boards and the distant hooting of owls set my nerves on edge. But fear, on top of the endless drudgery of housework, is exhausting and even my own terror was not enough to keep me awake. My old nightmares had left me, the ones that would wake me in a sweat. The ones where Mum, her face ashen and drawn, would be gasping for breath and the sound of the air in her lungs rattling would grow louder and louder while I stood frozen and helpless, reaching out but never able to touch her. The Ink had put a stop to them and since being infected my dreams had been of the marsh, the water sparkling and rippling through the creeks, the sea lavender blooming and the mud stinking as the marsh basked under the hot summer sun and I listened to the wild songs of the birds soaring far above me through the blue sky.

Chapter 17

"Wakey Wakey!"

I jerked out of my sleep, bolt upright.

"Sorry," Arnold laughed, "didn't mean to make you jump." The hot milk and honey in the cup in his hand slopped into the saucer as he sat down on the end of the bed.

"What are you doing here? You're supposed to be in London," I flopped back against my pillows, suddenly weakened by the relief of seeing his face.

"We got as far as Norwich and Charles changed his mind. So we put Miss Lamb on the train and spent the day looking round. Did a bit of shopping. The drive back was hair raising. The headlamps don't light the road that far ahead and with the mist — well, we just crawled along. It took ages. Didn't get back until half past ten. I looked in but you were sound asleep. You looked so peaceful I didn't want to wake you up." I groaned and sat up again, took the hot milk and honey from him and swallowed a large, restorative gulp. He folded his arms, "Did you have a good day?"

"No! It was awful. Mrs Egmore got drunk and then Mrs Bloggs turned up. She was sneaking round the house."

Arnold's jaw dropped, "No! Really? Nosy old baggage. You know what they say." I shook my head. "When the cat's away the mice do play," he chuckled, "or big rat in this case."

"Well you better not go away again then." I wanted to tell him about Ada and Tommy but I knew he'd never believe me. I took his hand like I used to when I was small, "Don't leave me here on my own — not ever."

He stood up and kissed my cheek, "Don't worry. Next time I'll make sure Miss Lamb's about — I doubt if Mrs Bloggs would take her on here — on her own patch. Anything else happen?"

"Mrs Bloggs bought a package for Mr Egmore. She thinks it's Miss Lamb's Christmas present. It's on the kitchen table."

"I shall deliver it to Mr Egmore personally," Arnold grinned and left the room. The warm bed, the hot milk and Arnold, the day couldn't have started better. I stayed there as long as I could, until Arnold shouted, "Get a move on, Zilla, I'm starving," as if he was incapable of finding his own breakfast. So I wriggled out from under the covers, dressed and drew back the curtains. A grey day. Mist cloaked the stables and yard in a dreary haze.

When Mrs Egmore eventually showed her face it was the same colour as the day, grey. The lines around her thin mouth looked even deeper than usual and her eyes were bloodshot. Any sympathy I had for her evaporated at the thought of cleaning her vomit encrusted dress. It disgusted me so much that it was worth trading chores with Mrs Pinkney, I would scrub the corridor floor and I could leave the dress for her to wash.

Mr Egmore must have had his suspicions about her. Dark eyed, unkempt and still in his dressing gown, he appeared in the corridor as she walked in through the back door, "Any alcohol, Mrs Pinkney?"

"No, sir, no alcohol," she looked surprised, surprised to see him and surprised by his question.

"Do you mind if I just check your coat?" She shot me a dirty look but shook her head and held her hands up as he patted her pockets. They were empty. "My apologies. Mrs Egmore has let herself down and I still can't find the source of the problem."

"Shame, sir. Terrible thing, the drink, but I can't help you I'm afraid," she hung her coat on a hook and waited until he'd left the corridor, heading back to the library. "Squeal, did you?" she snarled.

"Not me," I felt braver knowing Arnold was behind me in the kitchen stuffing his face with bread and marmalade, "maybe Mrs Egmore told him herself. Told him when she was drunk."

"Never. She won't give me away."

"She might do one day — when she's addled and can't think straight – then you'll be for it!" A minor victory. I swanned off, leaving her fuming with the sick stained dress in her hands.

It was late morning by the time I went out to fetch logs for the study fire. Mr Egmore prefers the smell of burning wood to coal. I filled the basket but couldn't bring myself to go straight back indoors. Being out in the fresh air, even cold, damp air, felt better than being cooped up inside so I dumped the basket by the back door and took a wander along the drive. Creakie Hall was in a world of its own. The trees wore the mist like a shroud, their limbs clothed in its ghostly vapour as they stretched skyward. The end of the driveway was lost to view but somewhere someone was humming cheerfully. As pale as a phantom through the haze, walking smartly towards me, carrying a bag in each hand, Miss Lamb appeared.

I ran along the muddy drive to meet her, "You're back! I didn't think you'd be back until six o'clock!"

"Good morning, Zilla. I am indeed — back. I caught the early morning train and as luck would have it Mrs Norton was at Norwich station about to board the train to Ipswich. She very kindly suggested that I return with her chauffeur. Can you imagine that?" Her voice trilled, "I sat on the front seat. It's so much more thrilling than sitting on the back seat. The countryside positively raced past until we ran into this dreary fog — we had to creep along for the last few miles."

"Did your visit go well?" I took one of her bags and she slipped her hand through my arm as we walked together, water dripping onto our heads from the wet branches above us.

"It was busy. Very, very busy. I completed all my errands yesterday and I simply couldn't face another day of shopping. One has to be so forceful at this time of year — so many people are trying to get the attention of the shop assistants — and the queues! It's undignified," she sidestepped a puddle. "Was yesterday bearable for you?"

"Mrs Egmore got drunk and I saw Ada and Tommy again. I can't tell Arnold — I know he won't believe me." We had passed the last wind-blasted tree and were following the path to the side of the house, towards the back door, when Mrs Pinkney appeared, looking shifty.

Miss Lamb stopped in her tracks. "Well now, what is she up to?" Mrs Pinkney looked from side to side, checking the coast was clear, but didn't spot us hidden as we were by the mist and the shrubbery. Two large stone urns stood either side of the gate to the yard and she bobbed down by one, slipped her hand around the back, pulled out another bottle of gin and slid it into her apron pocket. Miss Lamb beamed triumphantly, "Now I've got you!" Mrs Pinkney slipped back into the house and we followed. Even though she was surprised to see Miss Lamb her expression stayed the same, as if butter wouldn't melt in her mouth, "You're back early. London too exciting for you?"

Miss Lamb held out her hand, "The bottle of gin, if you please, Mrs Pinkney."

"What are you talking about — gin? I haven't got any gin."

"I just saw you take it from behind the stone urn by the gate. Don't deny it," Miss Lamb was in her element, victorious as Mrs Pinkney tasted defeat.

She handed the bottle over with a scowl, "Are you going to tell Mr Egmore? You know if the old woman doesn't get it from me she'll get it from someone else."

"No, I'm not going to tell him." Miss Lamb's answer hit me like a brick. My jaw dropped. "I could, but I'm not going to." She continued, "You are correct in saying she will get it from someone else. I am well aware that when Mrs Egmore wants alcohol she will stop at nothing to get her hands on it so if she doesn't use you as her delivery service she will use someone else. And the devil you know is better than one you don't." A trace of a smirk crossed Mrs Pinkney's lips but Miss Lamb wasn't going to let her get off that lightly, "There's a price for my silence. You will put a stop to this stupidity about Zilla not being allowed in the village. Don't pretend you don't know anything about it. You and Mrs Bloggs have cooked it up between you."

Mrs Pinkney shrugged, "It's not just us. The village don't want her."

"Where Mrs Bloggs goes the rest of the village is sure to follow. You will instruct Mrs Bloggs to welcome Zilla back into her shop —" Miss Lamb paused, "and I do mean welcome! Unless you want me to tell Mr Egmore."

A sly smile teased at the corners of Mrs Pinkney's mouth, "Don't forget I know their little secret about old Mr Henry."

Miss Lamb didn't even flinch, "So do I and if that little secret gets out I shall make sure that everyone knows you were the one to tell it. You are paid by Mr Egmore and you live in Mr Egmore's property by his grace and favour. I presume being homeless has no appeal for you." She didn't get an answer but Mrs Pinkney's silence spoke volumes. "Good. Zilla and I will be visiting the village tomorrow morning. I do not anticipate any unpleasantness."

"If that's what you want," Mrs Pinkney was churlish in defeat. "If I was her I'd be on the first train away from here."

"Fortunately, you are not her." Miss Lamb smiled broadly at me, "the moment I met Zilla I knew she was exactly the kind of young woman that Creakie Hall needs. And if we all work together to create an amiable atmosphere I sincerely hope she'll stay."

And stay I did.

Chapter 18

Mrs Bloggs did not look happy. She shuffled behind the counter, her lips puckered, the taste of defeat very sour, "Good morning, Miss Lamb. What can we do for you today?"

"Good morning, Mrs Bloggs." Miss Lamb moved away, feigning an interest in a display of biscuit tins, "Zilla has our list. Perhaps you'll be good enough to assist her?"

Mrs Bloggs bulky frame twitched, "Well?"

As I held out our list I couldn't keep the grin off my face, "Good morning, Mrs Bloggs, isn't it a lovely day?"

Her mouth tried to smile sweetly but her eyes were still looking daggers, "I'm far too busy to take any notice of such things. Give me that!" She snatched the list away and, huffing and puffing, made short work of finding everything. "Will you be paying today or do you want it all on account?"

"On account, as usual," Miss Lamb said sweetly. The doorbell rang and three women entered, their faces agog with surprise as they hovered by the door whispering, "She's back," "After all Mrs Bloggs said she's let her in the shop again," and, "I don't know what to make of it. Do we say something? Do we ignore them?"

Slightly unnerved I stuffed everything into the basket as quickly as I could but Miss Lamb was in no hurry. An eyebrow was raised in Mrs Bloggs direction.

Her words burning like bile in her throat Mrs Bloggs said, "It's nice to see you back again, Zilla. Good day, Miss Lamb." Red-faced, she hollered, "Lucy, where the devil are you, girl? Get in here, NOW!" And with undignified haste she retreated into the store room.

But Miss Lamb wasn't quite finished and after wishing them all a polite, "Good morning," the women had also been forced to acknowledge me before we left. The bell rang cheerily as I shut the door behind us. Miss Lamb beamed victoriously, "That's cooked her goose!" There was a spring in her step as we walked past all the cottages and houses on the way home, their curtains twitching, word would be out, carried along the village grapevine. I was back.

It took a few days for the staring and the whispering to stop, not completely, but almost. My daily walks to the village shops were always under thick layers of cloud. The winter gloom seemed never-ending.

Sometimes drizzle fell, seldom enough to leave a puddle but just enough to keep the driveway muddy.

Christmas Eve arrived but barely seemed to touch Creakie Hall. Will cut some greenery, holly and yew, at Miss Lamb's request but Mrs Egmore refused to have it in the drawing room, "It harbours insects and stains the paintwork." So we decorated the kitchen and I put a bunch of holly in the window of my room. The red berries looked so jolly. It was late afternoon when Miss Lamb sent me to Mrs Bloggs for a packet of Fry's Cocoa and a jar of Golden Shred marmalade. Since being infected with the Marsh Ink I'd developed a taste for it and she was concerned that we may run out over Christmas. The spirit of the season had affected Mrs Bloggs deeply and she actually sounded like she meant it as she wished me, "Merry Christmas," and allowed Lucy a minute to chat. The sun had dropped behind the woodland and the daylight had almost faded away as I passed Ivy Terrace. On the opposite side of the road Ezra and a pasty-faced friend were leaning against a wall, kicking at a tussock of grass on the verge. "Here she comes. How's your face, Zilla? Still wriggling?" I didn't answer. Mum always used to say, “Don’t speak. You’ll only encourage them. It’ll only make them worse,” whenever I was teased at school. Ezra started to laugh, “How about a Christmas kiss, Zilla?”

His friend spat into the road, “Urgh! You wouldn’t want to kiss her — you’d get a gob full of black snot!” They both fell about laughing as if it was the funniest thing ever. “Oi! Snot face, we’re talking to you.” I didn’t answer but I picked up the pace, walking faster. “Rude, isn’t she — ignoring us!” They both left their spot by the wall and crossed the road behind me. My nerves were on fire. Should I run? Should I turn round? I didn’t know what to do so I held my head up and kept walking, knuckles turning white as I gripped the handle of the basket. They were catching up. Then they were right behind me, “Didn’t you hear me? I said, snot face, we’re talking to you!” Ezra’s hand grabbed my arm but he let go just as fast, squealing, “OW! That hurt!”

“Good! It was meant to.” I spun round to find Will’s dad, Mr Flack, behind Ezra. Ezra had his hand to his head, holding his ear, whining. Mr Flack raised his hand again, “Now bugger off, the pair of you! Don’t let me catch you up to no good again — d’you hear me, boy? Or I'll be having words with your father." The two boys mumbled, backing off, but not fast enough for Mr Flack's liking, "GO ON, BUGGER OFF!" he shouted.

As I watched them retreat to the safety of the village green Mr Flack asked, "Are you all right, girl?"

I nodded, thankful that he couldn't see my knees were shaking underneath my skirt, "Yes, thank you, Mr Flack."

He adjusted his cap on top of his thinning white hair, "Nasty little sod that Ezra. If you have any more trouble just give us the word and I'll send Will round to sort him out." I didn't like to think what that might mean so I didn't ask but just thanked him again. "How's things up the Hall? I hear Millicent's finally got the better of Mrs Bloggs."

It had never occurred to me to ask Miss Lamb's name so it came as quite a shock, "Millicent? Miss Lamb's name is Millicent?"

He chuckled, "It is. Me and Millicent we go way back. She was quite the girl when she came here — so many years ago it don't bear thinking about. Come on, I'll walk you home." Even though I'd seen Ezra and his friend walk away I was afraid that they might have sneaked back and would follow me as soon as I was alone. So I didn't say no, didn't say that I could manage, because I didn't feel I could. It was a slow walk, Mr Flack happy to talk, as the last of the daylight faded and evening drew on. "Mrs Pinkney been giving you any trouble?"

"A bit," I wasn't sure how much I should say.

"She's not a happy woman. You know it was her little brother Tommy that got infected with the Ink — just like you got infected."

I didn't know. "Tommy Cottle?" I was amazed. Miss Lamb had never mentioned it, neither had Mrs Pinkney.

Mr Flack shook his head sadly, "He was a bright little chap, happy sort. Always on the move. Always running about. Right useless at school — couldn't bear sitting in a chair. Used to play hide and seek behind those old trees on the driveway with young Mr Egmore. Right pair they were. Always getting into scrapes." The clouds parted, leaving the moon unclothed, "Hannah was heartbroken when he died. Thought the world of her little brother, she did." With the last houses of the village behind us the marsh spread away to our right, the pale creeks and pools magically reflecting the moonlight, wild geese honking loudly as they settled down for the night. “Have you seen him?”

“Tommy?”

“That’s right, Tommy. I seen him on the marsh sometimes. Gives me chills it does. You can see right through his hands and feet now. He’s fading away, extremities first. Says he’s waiting for his mother … poor child.” I didn’t want to answer. But he’d already guessed. “So you have seen him then. I thought you had. Both of you being infected like. Not everyone believed me when I told them I’d seen him. Suppose that’s fair enough — ghosts ‘n’ all. Tommy weren’t born here. He was Mrs Cottle’s youngest. She got a letter from her sister in Yarmouth. She’d been taken poorly so Mrs Cottle went off to help out and when she come back she was carrying Tommy in her arms. Hannah, being the oldest, went with her to help out, she were sixteen at the time. Gone nearly five months they were.” We reached the end of the driveway and he stood for a while taking a long look at the house. Dim lights glowed feebly in the windows. Miss Millicent Lamb had lit the oil lamps. “You wouldn’t think it possible for four walls to hold so much misery. Most of it they brought on themselves.” He didn’t seem to feel the cold and lingered but I was frozen and desperate to get indoors. Eventually he took his gaze away from the house, "Well, here we are then, Zilla, you be all right from here?"

"Yes, thank you, Mr Flack," I answered, already a few paces away from him up the driveway, "and thank you for helping me."

"That's all right, girl. You have any more trouble you just let us know." He waved and turned back towards the village, "Merry Christmas!"

"Merry Christmas," I called back as I hurried away between the wind-blasted trees. The moonlight faded away, smothered by cloud. In the darkness I was unable to see clearly where I was going and had to slow down, trying not to slip as I picked my way over the mud. The hairs on the back of my neck stood up, someone was watching me. I shot a look behind. No one was there, not Ezra, nor his friend, but as I passed the last tree Tommy's ghostly face peeped out from behind the trunk.

"Zilla," his whisper carried to me on the cold air.

I wasn't frightened of him anymore, "Tommy, what are you doing there?"

"I got a new rhyme. I made up. D'you

want to hear it?" He stepped out from behind the tree, hopping from foot to misty, bare foot.

"Go on then. But be quick I'm freezing."

"Bye Zilla Bunting, the beast has come ahunting, sneaking in the night, it'll give you such a fright — I made it up all by myself! It rhymes don't it," he said with pride.

Somewhere in the shadows I heard Ada laugh, a strange sound, its fine threads twisting around the tree trunks, drifting up into the night sky.

That's when I knew it was Mrs Bloggs. The beast had to be Mrs Bloggs, sneaking in the night. From then on I was on my guard.

Chapter 19

Christmas at Creakie Hall was dull. At least I thought it dull. Miss Lamb was quite chirpy. Her Christmas was devoted to the suffragettes. When Arnold had said he was going to London I'd given him strict instructions to buy six good-quality, white cotton ladies handkerchiefs for Miss Lamb's Christmas present and even though he only got as far as Norwich he did actually remember to buy them. When I'd had a couple of hours to spare I'd embroidered small flowers in the corners in two of her favourite colours, purple for the royal blood that flows through the veins of every suffragette and green for hope. I don't think she had been given many presents in her life because she was smiling all morning and displayed them on top of the chest of drawers in her room as if they had great value. Mr Egmore gave her an enamel brooch with the words, 'Deeds Not Words,' picked out in purple. It had been in the package delivered by Mrs Bloggs. I don't know what Mr Egmore gave Arnold but it was delivered behind closed doors and left Arnold with a sly grin on his face. I didn't even want to ask.

Miss Lamb gave me a small box and when I opened it I found a shiny, silver bicycle bell. "Once you have a bicycle you can spread your wings and join the local club. A young woman of the twentieth-century can achieve all sorts of things if she's a mind to." I had spotted an advertisement for a bicycle in one of Miss Lamb's periodicals and had set my heart on it. And her gift set me thinking, a fanciful, wishful kind of thinking, that maybe Mr Egmore and Arnold between them would give me enough money to buy a bicycle. But Mr Egmore gave me a one pound note. I should have been grateful, one pound is a good deal of money. I had thought that he might have been more generous seeing as I had been infected on his property and by the Ink in his father's book but then I felt a bit guilty for being so greedy on Christmas Day. He said it was from Mrs Egmore as well but when I thanked her she didn't know what I was talking about. Arnold gave me a blue scarf. I suspect Miss Lamb had a hand in buying it and may have brought it back with her from London but however it had reached him it was lovely.

By New Year's Eve my ambitions regarding a bicycle had been set and I made a resolution to put all my Christmas money towards the purchase of a top-quality bicycle, not the cheaper one that I had been thinking of. Miss Lamb would put money saved from my wages into a tin every week and by the summer I would have enough for a top of the range Rudge-Whitworth. We'd found an advertisement promising reliability, safety and excellent quality. It made no mention of speed or escape which appealed to me far more than anything else. I snipped the advertisement out and pinned it on the back of my bedroom door. With my head full of dreams of peddling along the summer lanes between banks of white cow parsley under blazing sunshine I picked up a tray and headed for the dining room to collect the dirty china used at lunch but came to a dead stop in the hall as an argument in the drawing room reached fever pitch.

I thought at first Mrs Egmore had been at the drink again but she was sober, shouting, "You should make them go. If you cared as much as you claim to you would make them go!"

"They are happy to stay —" Mr Egmore tried to get a word in.

"As if having to tolerate your unnatural, disgusting proclivities is not bad enough behind closed doors you would have them tainted by association with this house. The whole county will shun them. This family has no social standing left — our name is mud — we have no connections left."

"And whose fault is that! As you well know that has nothing to do with my proclivities as you call them — which, I should add, are completely natural and healthy — but everything to do with you! No one wants to be connected to a drunk."

"A drunk I may be but you are sober and missing the point. They will never be able to get work elsewhere if they stay here any longer."

"Bunting doesn't want to work elsewhere."

"And what of Zilla? What's to become of her? She can never be truly safe here — never! The boy Cottle and poor Ada are testament to that."

"Their deaths had nothing to do with the Marsh Ink," Mr Egmore barked, "you're being ridiculous! Irrational!"

"Don't use that tone with me. She would be safer away from here. She should be dismissed."

"Safer? She'd be safer without the Ink certainly. Dr Latham is coming for a consultation within the week. He was highly recommended by Dr Holman. His reputation is first-class. He may be able to remove the Marsh Ink from her face."

"Good! I want it back. It's worth a fortune and it belongs to us — not her! If I could cut the damned Ink out of her myself I would do it today and sell the cursed stuff. I'd leave YOU here to wallow in your own filth." She reached screaming pitch, "And what if he can't get it out? Have you thought of that? God knows she is no beauty but what looks she had are ruined. Her face is an abomination — a disaster! She's only fit for a freak show!"

From the gilt-edged mirror across the hall my reflection stared back at me, hair pulled tight back, winter white face stained grey with Marsh Ink. I had grown used to it, grown used to its colour, grown used to its funny little sensations, grown used to its happy dreams, but her words hit home. The corridor walls flew past me, the tray was thrown into the scullery, coat grabbed, door slammed and I was off, sobbing as I bolted across the yard. Putting as much distance between myself and the Egmores as fast as I could I ran up the track, along the edge of the wood and up the hill behind the house until I was out of breath and had to slow down. "Oh Mum … I wish you were here. I wish you hadn't died. If you hadn't I wouldn't be in this mess." I pulled the pins out of my hair, letting it fly around my shoulders and kept walking. A sharp wind was blowing, finding every gap in my clothes, cutting through my coat, chilling my stockinged legs above my boots. Finding shelter by a dense patch of scrub I sat down on the roots of an old oak and leant my back against its broad trunk, pulled out my handkerchief and blew my nose. "No good crying, Zilla," I told myself, "can't change any of it now. The Ink's stuck in your face and you'll just have to live with it." But giving myself a good talking to doesn't always work. It's not the same as when Mum gave me a good talking to, or Mrs Sowter. I wouldn't have minded living with the Marsh Ink if it had gone somewhere other than my face, somewhere out of sight, my stomach, my knees, my internals. Then no one else would ever know about it. "You've just got to make the best of it," I said out loud, thinking that I could only be heard by the pigeons and the gulls wheeling overhead.

"It's not that bad," Ada's voice whispered in my ear. "You still got lovely hair." Taken by surprise, I pressed myself back into the trunk of the tree as her face drifted in front of mine. "You ain't ugly,

Zilla."

How could I take the word of a ghost over the words of the living but then again, why shouldn't I? "Mrs Egmore says I am." Too miserable to be scared of her I wiped the handkerchief across my eyes trying to stem the flow of tears.

Ada snorted, "That old cow! Don't you take no notice." The air between us, although cold, wasn't freezing as she faded away. But her words still scattered like dried leaves caught in a breeze, "Don't listen to her … Don't trust her … She's poison."

My fear of Ada had faded, my heart didn't pound, my breath didn't stop, and I found myself wishing that she was still with me, the company of a ghost better than none at all. "See, Zilla Bunting, Ada doesn't think you're ugly. Now stop crying — the world hasn't ended." Talking to myself again I sniffed and stared hard at the horizon where a vast sheet of pale cloud met the steely blue line of the sea. Even from that distance I could almost taste the salt in the air when I licked my lips and smell the seaweed. The marsh spread far out to left and right, a sodden barrier between the wide, sandy beach and the village with its orange roof tiles and cobbled walls. Creakie Hall stood all by itself, half hidden by the trees, a forbidding, dour lump of a house. I looked down onto its hard brick walls, dead eyed windows and watched the smoke puffing out of the chimney pots and curling away on the wind. A blackbird's frantic alarm call alerted me to the sound of voices, men's voices coming along the track. Arnold and Will.

"Zilla! Zilla!" Their shouts carried across the field but for a minute I didn't answer, not wanting them to see me red-eyed from crying. "Zilla! Zilla!" As they drew closer the sudden worry that no one would ever find me overwhelmed the feeling of not wanting to be found and caught between the two emotions I found myself shouting back, "I'm here! Arnold, I'm here!"

They appeared around the side of the scrub patch, faces full of concern, "What's wrong? Miss Lamb said you'd run out and Will saw you run across the yard. What's wrong?" If Arnold had been angry with me I could have kept my tears bottled up but hearing the worry in his voice they flooded out again.

"Everything," I blubbed, "Mum … my face … and Mrs Egmore's been nasty."

He sat down beside me, putting his arm around my shoulders and pushing away my hair as it blew across his face, "What has she said?"

Between the sobs I blurted out, "That I'm only fit for a freak show. Everyone thinks I'm ugly."

Will squatted down on my other side and leant his back against the tree trunk, "I'd say you're a long way from ugly. I'd say a lot of men would be only too happy to walk out with a girl as pretty as you."

Arnold nodded, "Will's right. Bit of a mark like that isn't going put off the dedicated sort. And there's a lot more to you than just your face." He rubbed my arm affectionately, "Now if you had a face like Mrs Egmore I'd be worried. We'd have to call you Zilla the toad girl — it's the way she smiles that frightens me."

Will laughed, "Have you ever seen her eat a fly? She just sticks her tongue out and —" he stuck out his own pink tongue and whipped it across his lips, "Lovely!"

Arnold chuckled and pulled his handkerchief out of his jacket pocket, swapping it with my wet one, "As if I'd let my sister be put in a freak show!" He waited while I wiped my eyes, "Then again it depends how much money she could make. If it was two pounds a week I might reconsider."

I dug my elbow into his ribs, "OW! Maybe three pounds a week then."

I blew my nose on Arnold's handkerchief, "She says we'll be tainted by association if we stay here."

Will shoulders began to shake, a chuckle started in his throat and erupted into loud laughter.

"What? What's so funny?" asked Arnold. Both of us were bewildered.

"You haven't heard? About the little scandal?"

"No," we both said together.

"About seven years ago her and Mr Egmore went off to one of them big county balls. It's all going well until she has too much to drink and to cut a long story short ends up in the arms of some high and mighty lord — I forget his name — his wife finds them and they have a right old set to in the middle of the ballroom. Mrs Egmore was swearing and cursing. Just make matters worse she's as sick as a dog all over the floor." Will wheezed, "I'd love to have been a fly on the wall at that one! All her airs and graces and when it boils down to it she's a right old drunk. That's why the Egmore name is mud with the county set. It's why none of them come calling. She blotted their copybook — and the county really know how to hold a grudge. Tell any one of that lot that you work for the Egmore's and they'll turn their noses up at you good and proper. So next time she's nasty, Zilla, you just picture her in her ballgown, drunk as a lord and flat on her face." He stood up, still chuckling, "Come on, it's bitter up here. Let's get down to the house. Miss Lamb will've put the kettle on. You know what she's like — any crisis needs hot sweet tea to make it better — or hot milk and honey in your case." He held his arm out to me, "Madam, would you do me the honour?"

I managed a feeble smile, took his arm and, with Arnold on my other side, trudged back along the path, back to the gloom and the ghosts and the awful Mrs Egmore, back to Creakie Hall.

Chapter 20

The grease paint had not been the success that Miss Lamb and I had hoped for. The first three days had been wonderful. It had hidden the Marsh Ink so well and I'd thought that even if no one could get it out at least it was disguised. But on day four my cheek began to itch. After a week it had come out in a rash and after that I was able to use it less and less, eventually having to give up altogether, the merest dab producing spots the size of mountains. So it was with mixed feelings that I waited for the arrival of Dr Latham.

My stomach churned over as a big, black car rolled up the driveway. The chauffeur opened the back door and Dr Latham hopped smartly out into the drizzle carrying his leather holdall. Small and dapper with a bald head and spectacles he marched briskly towards the front door. Miss Lamb who was waiting, poised in the hall with an umbrella in her hand, just managed to open the door before he reached it and he walked straight in without having to knock. The agonising minutes dragged into half an hour as I waited to be called into the drawing room but the moment finally arrived and they were all waiting for me, Mr and Mrs Egmore, Dr Latham and Arnold.

After the briefest of introductions he asked if Arnold would give his consent to my treatment — as if I'm not capable of making up my own mind. The Ink was inside me but I knew it wouldn't be my decision. I was too young. If I'd been over twenty-one it would have been different. I could have told them to leave me alone, that I didn't mind having the Ink anymore. I was never poorly and it had stopped my nightmares and as far as I was concerned both of those things were definite advantages. It would have been nice if it could have moved out of my face, out of sight but I was learning to live with it.

Dr Latham smelt of tobacco and carbolic soap. He held a magnifying glass up to my cheek, "Hmmm." He poked at the Ink stain with his bony fingers, "Very unusual. Very unusual indeed."

"Can you do anything?" Mr Egmore stared intently, closely following Dr Latham's every move.

"Hmmm. Possibly. I do believe we can drain it out. It would only take the merest snick. I take it there's no objections." His voice was vague and distant.

The blood drained from Arnold's face, "I'll just wait in the … in the …."

I nodded at him. Better he wasn't there at all than laying on the carpet in a dead faint. He smiled back feebly but gratefully as he hurried for the door.

"Will it be possible to retrieve the ink, Doctor? It is very valuable and we would like it back," Mrs Egmore had a sickly smile on her face, sounding more smarmy than charming.

Dr Latham nodded, "I can't see why not. We can contain both the blood and the ink in one vessel and separate them later."

Mr Egmore's eyebrows almost met in the middle as he frowned, "That won't be necessary, Dr Latham, we will be destroying the ink as soon as it is removed." Mrs Egmore's chin stuck out, her face scrunched up in fury.

"If you'd like to wait outside," Dr Latham gestured airily to the door and they obediently left the room. But the closed door was not enough to keep their voices out as an argument started in the hall over the value of the ink. Mrs Egmore fought for it to be saved and Mr Egmore battled for it to be destroyed. None of it seemed to affect Dr Latham, absorbed in his work, as he asked me to lie on the couch. Anticipating his actions Miss Lamb had left a large towel for me to rest my head on. He rubbed something on my cheek, claiming that it would numb it. I had to fight every instinct to flee. My whole body wanted to escape. I was so frightened of the knife, believing that if I did see it I would run and Dr Latham would be flattened in the process. Averting my eyes I looked out of the window only to see two pairs of pale, dead eyes staring back at me. Tommy and Ada were peering in, mouths open, their eyes wide with fascination. Terrified as I was by Dr Latham and his knife their familiar faces were oddly reassuring.

He murmured, "Now … young lady … this is going to happen very quickly … Try not to move."

I caught a glimpse of a silver chain as his left hand pressed it down hard onto my cheek and forehead, circling the ink. "OW!"

"Don't move!" Dr Latham snapped. Ada and Tommy winced. A sharp pain seared across my cheek as he used his dreaded knife and my head jerked back. "I said don't move!"

I didn't move again. But the Marsh Ink did, squirming away from the silver chain. Like a worm evading the early bird it squeezed and wriggled behind my nose, oozing into the back of my throat, moving like a congealed lump of Miss Lamb's gravy, forcing me to swallow, gulping it down. I pushed Dr Latham hands away and covered my mouth with my hand, fearing I would be sick and it would all come out, Marsh Ink, breakfast porridge and hot milk with honey. Nothing happened, no gagging, no retching, but my mouth filled with the sweetest taste of strawberries which was bizarrely wonderful.

"Oh … How unfortunate … It appears to have moved." He sounded irritated as he settled his spectacles higher up his nose, "Are you aware of where it is now?"

I didn't reply for a moment, thinking quickly. If I said 'yes' he may want to examine that part, may even want to slice it open, so I said, "No."

"Hmmm … If you could open your mouth?" Unwillingly I opened it expecting him to see a slimy, black trail of Marsh Ink at the back of my throat but he shook his head, "Extraordinary … extraordinary. You may sit up." He took a small, folded pad of clean, white cotton from his medical bag and pressed it against my face, "Hold this until the bleeding stops," and then he left me sitting on the couch, picked up his bag and closed the door behind himself. I listened to him having muffled words with Mr and Mrs Egmore as I looked back at the window. Ada looked queasy but Tommy was pulling faces, fingers hooked into his mouth, pulling it back into a hideous grin. I bit my lip to keep a laugh in, knowing that if Mrs Egmore heard me I would surely be committed to the asylum. But deeper down the Marsh Ink wriggled defiantly in celebration of its narrow escape and instead of being disappointed that Dr Latham had been unsuccessful I found myself silently congratulating the Ink, even if only because it would annoy Mrs Egmore. Barely a minute had passed before I heard the sound of an engine and Dr Latham's chauffeur transported him away to other patients, other poor bodies for him to poke at and slice up.

Ada and Tommy snapped away as Mrs Egmore, wasting no time, was first back into the drawing room. Her face like thunder, "So where is the Ink now?"

"I don't know, ma'am. Somewhere inside."

"That much is obvious. I need it on the outside. It is worth a great deal of money," her lips puckered and she stalked across the room to look out of the window muttering irritably, "enough to get away from this god forsaken place."

With the Marsh Ink still celebrating inside me I was seized by a moment of cheekiness, "I think I just felt it wriggle, ma'am."

"Where?" she glared across the room.

"My unmentionables, ma'am, my down belows."

Her face puce with disgust she spat out her words "The insolence! Vulgarity is unbecoming even in a young woman of the lower classes!" Thwarted, she turned her back towards me, "If I could cut our Ink out of you myself I would cheerfully do so. But that — it would appear — is impossible. You may leave. Go back to the kitchen. Miss Lamb can dress the wound."

Still smirking and pressing the wad of cotton to my cheek I made a dash for the kitchen before she had a chance to change her mind and call me back. I caught Miss Lamb by surprise as she sat polishing the silver, "Finished already? Is the doctor still here?"

"No, he's gone. But he couldn't get it out."

"Of course he couldn't. I could have told them that — indeed, I did tell Mr Egmore that. But he insisted that some expensive doctor would know best — better than a middle-aged woman possibly could!" She pulled the cotton pad away from my face, "It's just a tiny cut. Nothing to worry about. It'll be healed over within a few days."

"Mrs Egmore is really upset."

"I'm sure she is. I was tidying Mr Egmore's study and found a letter. Of course I would never snoop but I couldn't help noticing it was a request for the Ink — offering twenty thousand pounds — imagine that — twenty thousand pounds!" It was no wonder that Mrs Egmore was angry. Miss Lamb stood back and a smile spread slowly across her face, "You're all pink again! Not a trace of Marsh Ink."

Hope bloomed within me, "Maybe it'll stay where it is … out of sight. Maybe it won't come back on my face again."

"Maybe," agreed Miss Lamb, "Time will tell."

As the day wore on her words kept coming back to mind, 'twenty thousand pounds — imagine that,' and I wondered if Mrs Bloggs knew how much the Ink was worth. Is that what she was searching for in Mr Egmore's study, a letter with a price?

But the next morning at first light I looked in the mirror and the Marsh Ink was back in its usual place, staining my cheek grey, but this time with a dark red scab slap bang in the middle of it. Instead of making my face better the doctor had made it worse.

Chapter 21

I'd dreamt it before but that time it felt real. I was flying high above the marsh, the sun warming my back, wind beneath me, lifting me up, carrying sweet scents that mingled with the hot stink of the mud. The miles and miles of green scrub had been transformed by purple drifts of sea lavender shimmering through the heat haze. The creeks and pools spangling the surface shone like mirrors reflecting the brilliant blue sky and all around me gulls cried, wheeling above a sparkling sea as it rippled along the wide expanse of sandy beach leaving behind a line of white froth. It was the dream of the Marsh Ink, the dream of its home. I'd never seen the marsh in summer so I knew it wasn't my memory but it was a happy dream, the kind you never want to end. But all things come to an end and I rolled over in bed and opened my eyes. I lay in the darkness listening to the night noises, the creaks and the groans of the old house, the whistle of the draught under the door and the occasional crackle as the last of the embers died down in the grate. Moonbeams shining through the gap between the curtains fell onto the patchwork quilt, brightly enough for me to see the starry pattern. "Zilla … Zilla," someone outside was calling my name. I slipped out of the bed and quickly hopped across the cold floor to the window. "Zilla … come and play with us … please," Tommy was standing in the yard, hair and clothes forever wet, waving his misty hands, "please, Zilla." He was just a small boy, a small, dead boy who was fading away and my heart went out to him as his voice broke like pins and needles against the glass, "We're playing hide and seek … I can't find Ada … I've looked everywhere … please, Zilla."

I nodded and waved back, tiptoed along the corridor past Miss Lamb's room, pulled on my boots and my coat and softly closed the back door behind me. Tommy stood in the brilliant moonlight, trickles of water running from his grubby shirt and short trousers, vanishing before it reached the ground. He was so eager to get started that he was barely able to stand still, "D'you like hide and seek? It's my favourite." He grabbed hold of my hand and as his translucent fingers touched mine I found they were cold but no longer freezing. I had lost my fear of ghosts. The icy barrier between us was broken. Hand-in-hand we ran across the yard through the deep shadows, out of the gate, and slowed to a walk along the driveway. The black branches of the trees stretched up, silhouetted against the night sky, casting intricate shadows over the rutted driveway. Tommy left me, running behind each gnarled trunk, hoping to surprise Ada but she wasn't there. He took my hand again as we passed between the old iron gates and reached the road, "She might be on the marsh … Mum says I'm not to go on the marsh but we could go and look … couldn't we … Zilla … please … please come with me."

"Come on then." We ran down the bank onto the muddy track, my boots slipping in the mud that never tainted his misty feet, the sound of his laughter drifting far over the winter green scrub. I followed him off the main track onto a narrow path and we walked alongside a broad creek, its water rippling as it flowed towards the sea, the reflection of the moon dancing on its surface. His blonde head bobbed along as he darted behind the clumps of tall reeds, their tatty, fluffy heads swaying gently but there was no sign of Ada. Some small animal on its nightly search for food rustled through the dried reed stems and somewhere far away a tawny owl hooted as it quartered a field. He stopped dead. His head drooping as he stared down into a wide pool, "This is where it done it."

"Done what?" I waited patiently for an answer.

His blond hair stirred, caught by a long gone, summer breeze that I couldn't feel, "The beast … I was playing hide and seek with Hannah when it watched me drown," his pale face turned up to mine, innocent eyes wide. He wrung the front of his grubby shirt with his hands, "I slipped in … I didn't mean to … I thought it was Hannah coming to help me out … but it was the beast." We stood quietly in the moonlight, both gazing down at the empty patch of water, no trace of its dark past showed on the surface, only our own pale reflections. "Big and black it were … Ada says it's wicked," he slipped his hand into mine. "I couldn't get out … and my face went under the water … and I was nearly gone and if it had give me a pull I could have got out but it just stood there and watched me drown … then it leaned over me and said, 'It's all for the best'."

"It's all for the best? — So the beast can talk then?"

He didn't answer but leant his head against my ribs, "Are you going to stay with us now?"

“She’ll stay,” Ada was standing behind us. “Should have gone when she had the chance,” her voice frayed like old fabric, its threads floating away across the marsh.

“D’you like the Ink?” Tommy left my side, “We liked the Ink … tastes of strawberries.” He started to giggle.

“Got to you, hasn’t it — the Ink.” In the emptiness of the marsh Ada looked smaller, more fragile, as if the slightest breeze could blow her away, “Like it got to us … you wouldn’t be without it now … like a friend inside.” I nodded.

“If you like you can play with us after you’re dead,” Tommy offered happily.

Ada grabbed him, tickling his sides, “Have to find us first, won’t she … your turn to hide.” He wriggled away from her, blond head bobbing as he ran along the path and disappeared behind a stand of reeds, his laughter fading away. Ada drifted closer to me, “Don’t let the beast get you too … like it got us … don’t let it get you, Zilla.” Her hair was loose, floating around her shoulders, “Wicked it is … wicked! Big and black … when it leans over you … it’s too late to cry for help … it’s too late to run away.” She was gone.

“I know who it is! It’s Mrs Bloggs!” I

called but no one answered. A beast that can talk, the only beasts I knew that could talk were human and it just confirmed my suspicions. Mrs Bloggs was the villain. She may have got Ada and Tommy but she wasn't going to get me. In the east a thin line of white broke the horizon and the wild geese started honking. I looked down to see thick mud squelching around my boots, caking the bottom of my nightdress. Ada was right, the Marsh Ink had got to me, the marsh felt safe, like home and I didn't want to leave it but her warning rung loudly in my ears. Certain that Mrs Bloggs wouldn't be on the marsh at that hour of the day I was in no hurry to get back to Creakie Hall and wandered slowly back along the path, running my hands over the soft reed heads, tatty from the winter winds. A curlew called beside me, the lonely sound burbling up into the light. There was no sign of Tommy and Ada or any other soul, living or dead, until I reached the road and heard the gentle clop, clop, clop of horse's hooves.

"Zilla!" Will called to me, "You all right?"

"Yes thanks, Will."

Duke came to a stop and Will jumped down from his seat on the cart, "What've you been doing?" He looked me up and down,

"Look at the state of you." Face full of worry he stared at the mud on my clothes.

"Just been walking."

"On the marsh? In your nightdress? In the dark? How long have you been out there?"

"Not long. Just needed to get away from the house for a bit, that's all." I lied to him, "I couldn't sleep so I went for a walk. I slipped. Wasn't looking where I was going."

Not looking entirely convinced but at least partly reassured his face relaxed slightly, "You want to be more careful — dangerous place at the best of times. Best get back indoors and cleaned up before anyone catches you. Mrs Egmore sees you like this she'll start thinking you've gone a bit —" he tapped the side of his head and I knew he meant mad. "Will you be all right? I'd stop but I've got to get to the station. Got to collect some boxes for Old Bag Bloggs."

"Don't worry. Honest, I'll be just dandy." I started walking up the driveway, "You get going."

He climbed back onto the cart, "Alright, but you get back inside and get warm." I listened to the steady clop, clop, clop of Duke's hooves as they faded away into the distance. The sky was light and I shivered in the morning chill. My mud caked nightdress flapped against my bare legs so I hitched it up and ran the rest of the way to the house thinking that it was far too early for anybody to be up, thinking that nobody would see me. But just as I reached the gateway to the yard Mrs Egmore's bedroom curtains twitched. I'd been spotted.

Chapter 22

Mrs Egmore eyed me up across the dining room table and smacked the top of her boiled egg with her spoon. "Why were you walking across the marsh so early this morning?"

I'd been rehearsing what to say if she asked and I was ready, "I couldn't sleep, ma'am, and I thought if I took an early morning walk at least I'd be feeling bright and wide awake for my duties."

Her eyebrows arched. Obviously she didn't believe me. "That's how the Ink took Tommy and Ada. They both became obsessed with the marsh. It was almost impossible for Mrs Cottle to drag Tommy away from it and Ada would be out at all hours walking on it whenever she got the opportunity. She should have been locked up for her own safety. Neither of them lived long after being infected." Her words unnerved me. Egg yolk dripped off her spoon and trickled down her chin, "Stay away from the marsh, Zilla, it is unhealthy. Control the Ink or it will control you — and that can only lead to terrible consequences."

"Yes, ma'am." I couldn't tell from her

voice if her words were well-meant advice or a threat. I settled on the latter as I waited on her, watching her eating breakfast. Her body was shapeless, still toad like despite her well laced corset. Wisps of hair escaped their pins and trailed down her back. Her jaws went round and round as her teeth mashed up bread and egg. She washed it down with tea and then dabbed delicately at her mouth with a napkin. Doubt had crept into my mind. Was I right in thinking the beast was Mrs Bloggs? On the marsh in the dark I had felt so certain but in the cold light of day my conviction seemed silly. What if Mrs Egmore was the beast and I was wrong about Mrs Bloggs? Perhaps it was neither of them. Perhaps it was someone else altogether. My thoughts were a riot of suspicion. Mrs Egmore took another sip of tea and leant forward to reach her book. Had she leant over Tommy and Ada as she waited for the ink to trickle out of them? Was Mr Egmore the beast? Had Arnold been deceived about his nature? Was Mr Egmore genuinely mad, bad and dangerous to know? I thought of his scruffy beard, long straggly hair and his eccentricities and decided that in spite of it all he was too decent, too proper. But the longer I stayed in the room with his mother the more unsettling I found her so I was glad when Miss Lamb bustled in with the morning shopping list.

I pulled on my coat and looked into the mirror by the back door to make sure my hair was tidy. Grey and pink, my reflection looked back. The dried scab on my cheek did nothing to improve my appearance and I said to myself, "A right mess you look, Zilla Bunting! Never mind, you'll have to do just the way you are. If anyone doesn't like it they better look the other way."

Mare's tail clouds, high and fine, whisped across the sky as I strode along the road through the chilly air. "Morning, Zilla," Mr Flack shouted to me from his front door as I passed his garden gate. He pointed up at the clouds, "Change on the way. Shouldn't be surprised if we get snow."

"Hope not!" I called back not slowing my pace, trying to avoid another conversation about the weather. I headed towards the butchers, scanning every bush, every shed, every cobbled wall in case the beast should be lurking behind it. My legs were working hard, my mind even harder, thoughts racing through it as to who the beast could be. When he was younger Arnold had collected all the tales of the great detective, Sherlock Holmes, by Mr Arthur Conan Doyle and he had allowed me to read one, on condition I took the greatest care of it. I did my best to bring some of Mr Sherlock Holmes powers of deduction to my situation. Could the beast be Mr Flack? Unlikely, I decided. Although I was sure that with all his children he could have made good use of the money from the sale of the Ink to improve their circumstances I didn't think money would have been the most important thing in his life, honesty probably mattered more and besides, he just didn't seem the sort. Bracing myself for the smell of raw meat I took a deep breath before I pushed open the door of the butchers. Ezra was behind the counter. Could he be the beast? No, he hadn't even been born when Tommy died. It had to be someone older. Speaking to each other as little as possible I asked him for stewing beef and mutton and he was wrapping them when, through the door at the back of the shop, I saw Mr Coe raise a chopper and whack it into a pig's carcass. I flinched, quickly turning my eyes away but then I saw the blood-soaked sawdust on the floor and I began to sweat. A cold, sick sweat that trickled down my back. Could Mr Coe be the beast? He was used to blood and butchery, used to handling dead animals and that was surely only a step away from handling dead people. Perhaps behind closed doors there lurked a very different man from the cheerful chap who stood behind the counter every day exchanging banter with all the women. With every blow of the chopper my fear grew. I grabbed my fourpence change from Ezra, stuffed the beef and mutton in my basket and left with as much composure as I could manage. Outside, my nerves in shreds, all I wanted to do was collapse on the ground in a heap but instead I steadied myself, took more deep breaths and headed for the bakery.

I looked at everyone with suspicion. Who could it be? Someone I knew or someone I didn't, perhaps it wasn't just one person, perhaps it was two, working together. I studied Mrs Turner in the bakery but with her gentle manner and white apron she seemed even less capable of murder than Mr Flack. I thought of Mr Turner. I'd only ever seen him away from the bakery twice and he had kept his head down, barely even mumbling a greeting. But his hands were extraordinarily large and hands used to kneading bread were surely strong enough to kill. But then no great force had been needed and how would he have got into Creakie Hall to reach Ada? No, it surely wasn't Mr Turner. Mr Bloggs was far too cheerful, too friendly and too obliging. But he was downtrodden and after years of being bullied by Mrs Bloggs perhaps he'd lost all control in a moment of madness and found himself alone on the marsh watching gleefully as Tommy drowned. But he would not have been able to reach Ada so he didn't seem very likely either. But Mrs Bloggs herself? The memory of her sneaking about Creakie Hall was uppermost in my mind as I waited in line at the grocery. I watched every tiny movement, every sour squint, the way she fingered the coins as she dropped them in the till and the way her pink tongue just poked out of one side of her mouth as she added up the money. And the way she sniffed when serving anyone she didn't like. Usually Lucy would climb the small set of steps to reach the top shelves but there was no sign of her and Mrs Bloggs had to do it herself. On the top step, holding onto a shelf with one hand, she leant over to speak to Mrs Rice in front of me and I pictured her in her black, shapeless coat leaning over Ada and Tommy whispering, "It's all for the best." Mrs Bloggs was definitely the most likely candidate and as I reached the head of the queue and faced her across the counter my tongue tied.

Her Christmas spirit had long since

faded away, in its place her usual grudging manner. "Cat got your tongue, Zilla?" She snatched the list from my hand and with barely another word to me stacked up a packet of Quaker Oats, a tin of Colman's mustard, a bottle of Brasso and half a pound of butter next to Fairy soapflakes for the washing. "On account?" She was blunt, even rude, and had shown me no mercy, no compassion, when I was infected but would that make her a killer, a murderer?

I nodded, squeaking, "Yes please, Mrs Bloggs, on account." She gave me a long, sideways look and sniffed as she took the ledger off the shelf, her eyes flicked to the Marsh Ink and back as she flipped to the right page, scribbled down the amount and snapped the ledger shut.

For a moment her attention rested entirely on my face staring at the grey Ink stain as, I imagined, she calculated its worth, then she snapped, "Is that all?" I nodded, unable to speak. "Well get a move on then! There's other people waiting to be served." Did the blood run cold through the veins of her heavy body I asked myself as I squeezed almost everything into the basket, tucked the packet of Quaker Oats under my arm and hurried for the door. I took a look back as she bent down to pick a cabbage from the box on the floor and made up my mind there and then. I was right. Mrs Bloggs was the beast. She was old enough, nasty enough and devious enough.

I was absolutely certain it was her until I reached Ivy Terrace. From the window of Mrs Pinkney's house one of her four blonde haired children pulled a face at me. Charming. Was Mrs Pinkney the beast? She was old enough, nasty enough and devious enough as well but would she leave her own brother to die? Mr Flack said she had been devastated when he died but had it all been an act? I remembered the day in the woods when I kissed Ezra. She had been there with dead leaves stuck to her back and her hair in disarray. What had she been up to? There was something strange about her, something hidden, something secret, but did it make her a killer? Did she have a guilty conscience?

The air grew colder as I wandered along the road. Maybe Mr Flack was right, maybe snow was on the way. Thoughts of the beast filled my mind and it suddenly occurred to me that it might have been one of the old staff, one that had already left. Maybe it was the cook who was running a boarding house in Cromer. Had she sold the Ink to buy the boarding house? Maybe it was the butler? Maybe he was bitter after years of looking at Mrs Egmore's miserable face and had decided to take as much of the Ink for himself as he could before running to London and selling it for a fortune. If it had been one of the old staff then I was safe — unless word had reached them of my being infected with the Ink and they were coming to find me. I had been so certain of Mrs Bloggs when I looked at her but the more I exercised my powers of deduction the more I doubted my own judgement and trying to think like Mr Sherlock Holmes wasn't helping to solve the problem. Unable to make up my mind my feet trudged on towards Creakie Hall and, as I scanned every tree trunk, every bush and every distant shadow, I found myself caught on the horns of another dilemma. If the beast was after me then I should leave immediately but as soon as I passed the last cottage and saw the marsh ahead I knew it was impossible. The marsh, like the Ink, had got under my skin, it was my home. But if I was going to stay how could I protect myself? The question rolled over and over inside my head — how could I survive when Ada and Tommy had not?

Chapter 23

I spent all of Sunday worrying about the beast. Half the day I was convinced that it was Mrs Bloggs and half the day I was convinced that it wasn't her. There was no sign of the Ink ghosts, Tommy didn't ask me to play and Ada didn't sing, so I had no one to quiz for facts. What had it looked like? What had it smelt like? How could I devise ways of thwarting it — even destroying it — with no information? Monday dawned with the grey-yellow light that means snow is on the way and sure enough by nine o'clock it arrived. Another Monday, another washday. Funny how the work I hated the most always seemed to come round so fast, like mathematics at school. Given the weather Miss Lamb decided that we should only wash essentials. My mud caked nightdress would have to wait. Steam filled the laundry room as Mrs Pinkney rolled up her sleeves and gently squeezed Mrs Egmore's silk blouse. But there was no pegging out. Instead, we hung it all on the racks indoors. In the warmth of the kitchen I picked up a tea towel to dry the plates and watched the snowflakes drifting down like tiny feathers, settling on the grass, slowly turning the lawn white. A cough, loud and sudden behind me, made me start.

Miss Lamb cleared her throat, "Why on earth are you so jumpy? It's like being with a nervous rabbit." Her eyes lit up as she laid her copy of 'Votes for Women' carefully on the kitchen table, "Listen to this, Zilla, a women's parliament will meet in Caxton Hall, London, on the eleventh, twelfth and thirteenth of February. To think of it — a women's parliament! The vote cannot be far away now — it simply cannot. To deny us any longer is grossly unjust."

"Would you like to go, Miss Lamb?" I asked, half distracted by thoughts of ghosts and beasts.

"Would I like to? I should dearly love to," she sighed, "but we are stuck here, in the back of beyond. London, my dear, is a world away."

"You could take a small holiday. Surely Mr and Mrs Egmore would part with you for just three days?"

Mrs Pinkney had heard us talking as she came into the room and pushed past me to reach the cupboard where the silver was kept, "Part with her? They wouldn't care if she never came back!" She took out a silver teaspoon and waggled it at Miss Lamb, "For

Mrs Egmore. She asked me to fetch it. Misplaced loyalty, that's what you've got, Miss Lamb, misplaced loyalty."

"Thank you, Mrs Pinkney, for your observation. Was there anything else?" Miss Lamb remained composed, refusing to be baited.

"No. You get back to your suffrage and votes. Work for old maids, that is. It's not like you've got anything else important to do with no husband and no children," she slipped the silver spoon into her pocket and flounced back to the corridor. "Not like the rest of us who've got better things to think about."

Miss Lamb gritted her teeth, waiting until Mrs Pinkney's footsteps had clicked the whole length of the corridor and the hall door had closed behind her, "Really! That woman! As if there's nothing more to life than husbands and children." She tapped the table with her forefinger, "I do hope, Zilla, that in this modern age you will not feel that you are worthless unless you are a wife and mother. There is so much to do — so much to be achieved — and women have the right to be a part of it just as much as men do." I pictured Miss Lamb, militant, defiant, marching towards Parliament with all the other suffragettes, dressed in white with a purple and green sash, brandishing her placard and wearing her 'Deeds Not Words' brooch. It made me smile and she noticed, "Why are you smiling? Is it amusing to think of women achieving great things?"

"No, Miss Lamb. I just think you should be with them. You're wasted here."

Her face glowed, "Thank you, Zilla. It's rewarding to know that you have a higher opinion of me." She picked up the letters the postman had delivered earlier and sighed, "Unfortunately we have work to do. London will have to wait."

The day dragged on and the snow continued to fall, drifting silently against the walls of Creakie Hall, magically hiding its drabness. At quarter to three I crossed the hall to the dining room to make up the fire. Under the snow filled clouds the grey afternoon light was fading away early and the long winter evening was drawing on. I closed the door behind me to idle away a few moments watching the snow, falling so softly, so peacefully, the pure flakes gently transforming the garden. It was hard to believe that somewhere out there a beast was lurking, a human beast, but a beast nevertheless. A slight chill made me shiver and Ada appeared, kneeling by the fireplace.

She struck a ghostly match, its cold flame flickering blue as she held it against paper and kindling that had long since burned away.

"Ada?" I knelt down beside her, speaking softly so no one else would hear me.

She looked up, "Don't let the beast get you, Zilla … not like it got me and Tommy."

"But who is the beast?" I knelt beside her.

"Don't know … but we can feel it coming. It's sniffing for you. You've got to run … tricked me it did … put gin in my tea … felt warm when it slid down my throat … 'cos it was only a little fall and I weren't ready to go … leaned over me and said, 'It's all for the best'… waited for the ink to run down my nose … wicked it was … wicked! … You haven't got much time left … it's coming for you … we can feel it coming … Tommy and me," her voice was worn out by time, its fine wisps dispersing in the still air.

"I don't want to leave — the marsh is my home now — and I've got nowhere to go." A door slammed in the hall and she was gone. I knelt, thinking of the gin in her tea and wondering if that was why she fell down the stairs. She had been too unsteady to stay on her feet, just like Mrs Egmore when she was drunk. I waited, hoping she would come back but after five minutes I gave up and banked up the fire. I took a long look out of the window, the fallen snow was almost an inch deep, and she appeared again, deathly pale, a wraith in a world of white. Finding nowhere to settle the snowflakes drifted through her body. Separated by the cold glass she stared back at me.

"Bye Zilla Bunting, the beast has come ahunting, come to get what's in your skin...." Her face twisted with misery and anger, her voice like pins striking the glass pane, "... Don't you go drinking no gin, Zilla, d'you hear me? Don't you go drinking no gin!"

I shook my head, "I won't, Ada — promise — promise I won't!"

Chapter 24

The snow was crisp on the ground and icicles had begun to form, hanging from the edge of the lean-to roof, as my feet crunched on all the old bits of bark lying on the ground. Woodlice scurried away as I grabbed logs from the stack and tossed them into the basket. In the half-light I kept looking over my shoulder, convinced that the beast would pounce on me at any moment. Had Mrs Bloggs left her shop and was lurking somewhere in the yard? Or should I be looking for someone else? I was desperate to get back indoors. "Zilla," a small voice whispered behind me.

I spun round, "Tommy! Don't sneak up on me like that. You gave me a fright."

He was grinning from ear to ear, "I got a new rhyme. Ada made it up. D'you want to hear it?" I shook my head. I'd had enough of Ada's rhymes for one day. He hopped from foot to misty foot, bursting to tell me, "Oh go on … please … I remembered it special for you."

I couldn't stand the look of disappointment on his face, "Better make it quick. I've got work to do."

He stood with his feet together, straight back, as if he was going to recite it proudly in front of the whole school, "Bye Zilla Bunting, the beast has come ahunting, with a bottle and silver spoon, 'cos you'll be dead soon."

"Tommy that's —" I was about to say 'horrible' but he cut my words short by vanishing. I don't know if it was the cold or his song that made me shiver but I snatched up the log basket and dashed for the back door. Inside the corridor I dropped the basket onto the floor and leant against the wall, taking deep breaths.

"Are you quite well, Zilla?" asked Miss Lamb, cloth in hand. I nodded, even though my knees were trembling. "Then stop standing about. The fire in Mrs Egmore's bedroom needs attention. You'd best see to it. She rang the bell half an hour ago. And tell Mrs Pinkney she should go home. The snow's getting heavier."

"No, it isn't," I scuffed the snow off my boots on the doormat.

"I know that. But anything that encourages that woman leave this house is worth trying." I picked three logs from the full basket and, with a sinking feeling, climbed the stairs and knocked on the door.

Mrs Pinkney opened it, "You took your

time."

"Well, I'm here now," I carried the logs over to the fire, "Miss Lamb says you'd best get off home. The snow's getting heavier."

"I'll go when I'm good and ready," she walked slowly across the room, running her hand along the back of the sofa on which Mrs Egmore sat facing the fireplace until she stood behind her mistress. They both watched me as I picked up the poker, stirred up the ashes and the last burning chunks of wood before putting my logs on top. Feeling their eyes boring into my back my face began to burn.

"Look at the state of her," Mrs Pinkney said softly, "that stuff creeping about her face is disgusting."

"And so very valuable," Mrs Egmore sniffed, "I'd say bad things happen to girls like that but it would appear bad things already have."

I was not going to cry or shout or get flustered. I was determined not to give them the satisfaction so I stood up slowly and faced them. "Will that be all, ma'am?"

My heart skipped a beat. Mrs Pinkney held the silver spoon she'd taken from the kitchen, gently tapping it against an empty bottle of gin, "Don't think I can bear looking at that Marsh Ink much longer. Just think what we could do with that, Mrs Egmore. We could leave here — go to the south of France — go anywhere. Someone ought to cut that out of her." My blood ran cold.

Mrs Egmore pulled another bottle of gin from behind a cushion on the sofa and held it up, "Time you took your medicine. Just a little sip." My heart began to thump as she got unsteadily to her feet holding the bottle out towards me, "Be a good girl and do as you're told. It so much better this way… It's all for the best."

In a split second I was out of the door, running along the landing, belting down the stairs, along the corridor, bursting into the kitchen, "Miss Lamb, Miss Lamb! It's them. They're going to kill me!"

Miss Lamb leapt to her feet. Her reading spectacles flew across the table, falling onto the floor, the lenses shattering. "What? What? Who? Who's going to kill you?"

My words tumbled out in panic, "Mrs Pinkney and Mrs Egmore! They've got a bottle and silver spoon. Ada said they would. They're after the ink."

Miss Lamb's expression was a mix of confusion and shock, "What? Now? Are you sure they're not just trying to upset you?"

"Ada and Tommy said the beast would come for me — it's them! It's them! Mrs Egmore and Mrs Pinkney. They're the beast. They're in it together. What am I going to do, Miss Lamb? You've got to help me!" Frantic, I couldn't stand still, jittering around the table, "I've got to find Arnold. I've got to get away!"

"Zilla! Zilla!" Mrs Pinkney's voice carried through the house. I held my breath, listening. Her heels clicked on the hall floor.

"She's coming, Miss Lamb, she's coming for me! What do I do?" My whole body shook.

"Come with me," Miss Lamb seized my hand and pulled me towards the back door. She grabbed both our coats and her bag from the pegs, opened the door and pushed me out into the snow. "Quickly, Zilla, quickly!" Yanking on her coat she scurried across the yard, through the gate and hitched up her skirt as she trotted through the snow beneath the black branches of the wind-blasted trees. I followed her, wishing she could run faster.

"Where are we going?" I jogged along beside her.

"Onto — the — marsh," she puffed, her breath like the smoke from a steam train.

"But what about Arnold? I need to find

him."

"First — we hide you — then I — will find — Mr Bunting. He is with — Mr Egmore — they went in the motorcar to see — a man in the next village — about repairs to one of — the cottages." Huffing and puffing she held my hand as she crossed the road onto the track across the marsh, "Don't worry — Zilla dear — you'll be safe now."

Chapter 25

Miss Lamb panted, "I'm too old for this — Zilla — I must slow down."

"We can't stop, Miss Lamb, they're after me! Hurry!" I jogged on hoping that she would keep up with me. The daylight was fading as we left the main path, following another as it wound its frozen way across the marsh, "They can follow us! They can follow our footprints in the snow!"

"They could but I hardly think it likely. I doubt if Mrs Egmore will be capable of walking onto the lawn let alone all this way and as for Mrs Pinkney — she won't come onto the marsh alone — especially not in this weather. They're as thick as thieves — the pair of them are ghastly, absolutely ghastly!" She skidded on the snow and I grabbed her arm to support her. We stood for a moment looking back at Creakie Hall. Far off in the distance the windows glowed faintly in the twilight. "Zilla my dear, we've both had a dreadful fright." She unclasped her small, leather bag and pulled out a tiny hip flask, "I always keep this handy. One never knows when one may have a nasty shock. Don't worry. There's no alcohol in it, purely herbal.

It'll help you recover your equilibrium." She took a mouthful and offered it to me. I took a good swig. Flavoured with rosemary and thyme it was strong and warm. "Over there," Miss Lamb pointed to a long drift of reeds almost a hundred yards away, "you can hide there while I fetch Mr Bunting. He should return with Mr Egmore within the hour. I'll wait for him at the bottom of the driveway, catch him before he goes to the house, and bring him here."

I pulled my coat tighter. We hurried on. I had almost reached the reed bed when my legs began to fail me, moving slower and slower, "It's no good, Miss Lamb I can't keep up. I don't know what's wrong with me. My legs — they feel so tired — so heavy. My arms — they're like lead."

She took my arm and helped me along. "It's what happens, dear, when you mix the merest hint of alcohol with the Marsh Ink. It acts as a paralytic. You'll just get slower and slower until you come to a complete standstill. Heart — lungs — they'll all fail you in the end."

Bewildered I said, "But I haven't drunk any alcohol. I never drink alcohol. I took the pledge. Mum wanted us to."

"Obviously an intelligent woman who

understood the dangers. But you have been deceived, I'm afraid. Unpleasant but necessary. You have just had gin from my flask. Only a mouthful but that's enough." At the water's edge the soft heads of the reeds swayed gently from side to side, shedding snowflakes as they hid me from the path. My legs wobbled then buckled and finally gave way beneath me. Miss Lamb helped me onto the ground. "Feeling weary? A little lie down, dear. That's what's needed now."

"No! No! It's too cold. I want to go back to the house. I'm not well, Miss Lamb, help me!"

"I'm afraid not. I can't have you running back to your brother. Think of Mrs Egmore and Mrs Pinkney waiting for you. No, dear, I simply cannot allow it and besides, you'll never reach Creakie Hall in this state."

"I don't understand." I tried to stand up, struggled up onto my knees and slumped back down again, arms hanging limply by my sides, "You're going to save me. You're going to save me from them."

"No, Zilla dear, you've got the wrong end of the stick. Mrs Pinkney and Mrs Egmore are trying to drive you away. They believe that if you stay at Creakie Hall you will die," she unbuttoned my coat. "They're right of course." She tugged at the cuff of my sleeve, pulling my left arm out, "Everyone will think you died of hypothermia — very believable on a night as cold as this — and it won't take long." She pulled the other sleeve off my right arm and dropped my coat on the ground, "Mrs Egmore already thinks you're slightly touched. Walking on the marsh at all hours … getting mud all over your nightdress. She thinks you'll be in the asylum with Mr Henry within the month. Stupid woman."

I'd lost all control of my arms and legs, "You can't do this. You're my friend … you can't want me to die." I tried to scream for help but only a feeble cry left my mouth like the call of a marsh bird, lonely and haunted.

"None of us want to die but we all have to in the end. It's a pity your end will be sooner rather than later as I really have grown quite fond of you. But you'll feel no pain and that's a blessing. So there really is nothing to fear." Miss Lamb pulled a pair of gloves from her bag and slipped them on, "I'm sure this must all seem jolly unfair to you but if life were fair I would be mistress of this house and Mrs Egmore would be doing the cleaning with Mrs Pinkney." She laughed, "Aaahh, those would be happy days."

"But my new bicycle — you're helping

me to get away — all you said," unable to hold my body up any longer I flopped down onto the snow.

"All deceit I'm afraid. I had to earn your trust. Necessary lies to keep you happy but I can't have you peddling away when you hold the key to my future. It's all happened rather sooner than I intended but a women's parliament, Zilla — isn't it marvellous! As soon I read it I knew I had to be there. One must seize the day! Mrs Pinkney and Mrs Egmore will shoulder the blame for your death. Mr Egmore and Mr Bunting will believe that they drove you out into the snow — your death will be the result of their nastiness and hypothermia. How wonderfully convenient!"

My whole body began to shiver, teeth chattering so violently I could barely speak, "I-I-I d-d-don't w-w-w-ant t-t-to d-d-die. H-h-he-elp m-m-me p-p-p-l-lease."

Miss Lamb paced up and down, rubbing her arms to keep warm, "You just lie still and it will soon be over. I need the Ink. I've spent years imagining every possible solution for getting the Ink out of that book. Then you came along and on that very first day, the moment you caught the sweet smell of strawberries, I knew you were the answer to my prayers. I would have sniffed you out sooner or later, I can always sniff out someone who will be useful to me, but you gave yourself away with those two little words. I'll always remember them 'Ooo strawberries'. You extracted all of the Ink from the book all by yourself … how fortuitous. Obviously given our age difference I can't just sit and wait for you to die. That would be a ridiculous notion — and we both know that your death is the only way to get the Ink out of you again." The snow drifted down so quietly and she sighed, "If I'm ever going to lead the fulfilling, exciting life I deserve — and heaven knows I've waited long enough — then selling the Ink is the only way I can raise sufficient funds. And since that letter arrived offering twenty thousand pounds, a king's ransom, don't you agree? — It has given a sense of urgency to my endeavours. How else could I achieve such riches other than by selling the Ink? I've copied down the name and address most carefully. It's my only way out. I do hope you understand that my actions are born of necessity." She leant over me, "You may not wish to hear all this but there is no one else I can talk to. It's one of the drawbacks of this kind of enterprise. No one to confide in. No one to tell of my successes. No one to discuss ideas with. Whom could I possibly tell of the things I've done? Only you, Zilla, because you won't be here much longer to pass my confidences on to anyone else."

She stroked my hair gently away from my face as I mumbled, "H-h-help me … p-p-p-please."

"There, there, don't distress yourself. At the moment of your death the Ink will slip out just the same way it went in."

The alcohol had done its work. My limbs laid like stone. I was unable to move, to even lift a finger and I was so cold, so very, very cold.

"Miss Lamb! — I never knew it was you," wide-eyed with shock Tommy's ghostly face appeared at her elbow. "Old Miss Mutton Chops! — You could have saved me — but you just left me to die! You're horrible!"

"That's what happens to nasty little boys who call me names. You got nothing more than you deserved."

His face screwed up, angry and hurt as he shouted, "Bye Zilla Bunting, Old Miss Mutton Chops has gone ahunting, slit your throat from ear to ear, to bleed the Marsh Ink out. — That's what she does, Zilla, she's wicked! That's what Ada says — you're wicked!"

"Stop exaggerating, Thomas Cottle, I made the nearest snick in your cheek. It was sheer coincidence I found you in the first place. I should explain, Zilla, when I realised the price the Ink could command I used to walk the marsh with a bottle and silver spoon in the hope that I could find some just as Mr Henry Egmore had. Silly little boy had slipped in a pool. He was almost gone. I simply waited. I didn't even snick his face until he was dead — well, almost dead. The Ink did not run out of the wound but out of Thomas' nose. Unfortunately it was such a trifling quantity that it would have provided barely enough funds for six months. I decided to retain it, keep it in reserve as it were, until the price increased." She stamped her feet, walking up and down as she confessed, "Goodness, this must be the coldest night we've had all winter — snow is so pretty, don't you think. It covers a multitude of sins. But I digress. Mr Egmore always leaves his letters lying around and over the years the price of the Ink in that book rose and rose so I bided my time, waiting for an opportunity to show itself. As luck would have it I was walking past Mr Reece's cottage one evening when, in a drunken stupor, he poured beer from his own bottle into the pig trough for his piglets. Presumably he thought the result would be funny — a fool if ever there was one. One of the piglets had been infected with Marsh Ink — they were always escaping the sty and running onto the marsh. As soon as the alcohol touched its lips it dropped dead and the Ink just wriggled out of its snout. The tragedy was that I was not in a position to catch it but it did provide a solution to the vexing question of how to get the Marsh Ink out of Ada. The tea I sent up to her as she lay in bed after her fall was laced with gin. I seized the moment! Humans don't respond in quite the same way as piglets. It just takes a little longer." She tapped her watch, "Speaking of which are you ready to give up the ghost yet, Zilla?"

"So that's how you done it!" Ada's voice crackled with fury, her ghostly hair flying around her face. "You tricked both of us! — We should have had our lives — We should have lived them out — had our loves and homes and babies — and you took it all from us!"

"Ada, do stop being such a bad loser! Frankly you were only infected with the Marsh Ink because you were a greedy little thief. I don't suppose for one minute you've told Zilla how you were infected," Miss Lamb glared at Ada. "How the tin with the book inside it was always kept in a locked desk drawer and you picked the lock — presumably a trick you picked up from some other unwanted child in that hell-hole of an orphanage. Not a skill I have unfortunately — you brought your fate on yourself. Then Mr Egmore put the tin into the safe and had I known the combination none of this would have been necessary. I would simply have stolen it years ago. The amount of Ink I retrieved from you still wasn't enough to secure my future. I had to wait — and wait — and wait. But patience is a virtue is it not? I deserve a medal for enduring all these years at Creakie Hall. But the reward is worth it."

Ada's voice cut through the air as sharp as needles of ice, "I'll haunt you! — Till the day you die I'll be by your side — You'll never be rid of me — You're evil — You do wicked, wicked things — And I'll never let you forget it!"

The cold had seeped deep into my body, all my muscles paralysed, as frozen as the ground I lay on, my breath barely a whisper as snowflakes drifted softly over my dress. Tommy leant over me, eager to please, smiling happily, "We can play when you're done with dying can't we, Zilla? … Hide and seek … please?" I felt him press his cold, wet, lips on to my cheek in a ghostly kiss and the Ink began to move, slithering slowly under my skin, sliding away, oozing down my nose.

Miss Lamb was delighted, "So soon? And you're not completely dead yet! It must be the cold. It was the middle of summer when Ada passed on. Clearly Marsh Ink is affected by temperature. I must make a note of it for my prospective purchaser." She knelt down beside me, took an inkwell and a small silver spoon from her bag and used the spoon to coax the Ink into the inkwell. "How very convenient. If I hurry I can catch the last train to London. Thank you, Zilla dear, you've been most obliging." She corked the bottle tightly, wrapping it neatly with the spoon in one of the handkerchiefs I'd given her for Christmas. Silhouetted against the darkening sky she loomed over me, big and black, a true beast. She sniffed and whispered softly, "It's all for the best." Totally helpless I watched as she trotted briskly away over the fallen snow, Ada following close behind, her ghostly feet leaving no footprints.

Snowflakes drifted down through the darkness so quietly, so peacefully, gently covering me with a blanket of purist white.

Tommy laid down next to me, his cold, white face pressed against mine, "Ada's not coming back. She's going to haunt Old Miss Mutton Chops until she dies. Wherever she goes. That's what she said when she died. She said, 'I'll haunt the beast till it dies — soon as I know who it is — I'll haunt them forever.' But I'm staying here. I'm waiting for my Mum." His face blurred into darkness and his voice faded away, "Can we play now, Zilla?"

Chapter 26

Tibbs found me. His hot tongue licked my face and spread dribble all over my nose. With the ink gone I was able to breathe again and I felt the blood start to move in my veins, just enough to keep me alive. Tibbs' barking brought Arnold running to my rescue, "Oh my God! Oh my God, Zilla, what's happened? What have you done?"

Mr Egmore was hot on his heels, "She's taken her coat off! She's frozen!" I felt him lift me off the ground. I knew it wasn't Arnold, he would never have the strength. But from that point on my memories are hazy. I remember being carried and I'm sure I heard Will's voice. I remember the warmth of the fire in Mr Flack's cottage and how it slowly brought me back to life. And I remember how they sat with me for hours until I was finally able to speak again. My first whispered words were, "Miss Lamb."

"Do not distress yourself, Zilla, I will find her for you," Mr Egmore said kindly, "we all know how attached you've become to her. I shall bring her here immediately." But when he reached Creakie Hall he found Miss Lamb was long gone along with the Marsh

Ink, the rest of the silver spoons and the money that I had saved up towards a bicycle.

The Marsh Ink's legacy was a cast-iron constitution and within a fortnight I was back to scrubbing, dusting and cooking. No longer maid-of-all-work I was the new housekeeper of Creakie Hall. Another Monday, another washday, and as Mrs Pinkney rubbed extra soap flakes into Mr Egmore's shirt she asked me, "Did you ever see our Tommy? I thought with you being near dead and all you might have seen him."

I hesitated. I was never able to tell Arnold the truth about that snowy night on the marsh because he resolutely refused to believe in ghosts but I was not about to confide in Mrs Pinkney, "No."

"Only some in the village say they've seen him. I go looking in the woods but I've never seen him — not even once." For a moment she let her guard down and her eyes betrayed the truth, he was her secret shame and her great joy, her illegitimate son. "If only I'd been there … if only I'd found him sooner … my poor, dear boy."

So the days turned into weeks, the weeks into months, the months into years, and nothing was heard of Miss Lamb, no whispers, no rumours, until today when I opened the newspaper to see a photograph of suffragettes marching through London and there she was, dressed in white, defiantly brandishing her placard. As I looked at her image all the unanswered questions that had haunted me so often resurfaced. How could she have been so cold, so calculating? Had she seized the moment on that fateful day when Lucy came calling to suggest to the drunken Mrs Egmore that it was the perfect moment to look at her mother's sapphire necklace, knowing that Mrs Egmore would open the safe, knowing I would be drawn to the Marsh Ink like a moth to a flame? She was wicked. There were only two things that I learned from Miss Lamb, the first is that women's suffrage is a cause worth fighting for. Women are equal to men and we deserve the vote. The second thing is that betrayal is cruel.

I often see Tommy running alone across the marsh, his blond head bobbing along between the clumps of reeds and sometimes when the summer nights are long and warm we play hide and seek, his ghostly pins and needles laughter always giving away his hiding places.

With the Marsh Ink gone my face returned to its usual pink, no trace of it left, no stain to mark where it had been. But for many months I missed its funny little sensations, its strange happiness, and most of all I missed the dreams of flying high above the marsh with the gulls, so high I could see the pools reflecting the blue sky, see the wide, sandy beach and the white horses racing across the sea.

I walk on the marsh most days, to feel the freedom of the wide open space, to feel the wind on my face and listen to the cries of the birds, lonely and wild. It is my home. I will not leave it. I belong to it and love it dearly.

To this day the Marsh Ink has never been found but, dear reader, if you should ever be looking at a page and the captivating scent of strawberries fills you up with summer try not to close your eyes … and if the words begin to move ….

About the author

Bex Archer spent years drawing archaeological finds and illustrating children's books and magazines before turning to writing. Inspired by a niece with a love of vampires and all things spooky she wrote 'Four Dragon's Daughters'. Having been bitten by the writing bug she went on to finish the series drawing upon bits of history, Anglo-Saxon, Celtic and prehistoric, that had worked their way into her memory. 'The Ink Ghosts' is her first book for adults, young, old and any age in between. An enthusiastic photographer with a love of brilliant colour she uses her own photos to make short animations.

Thanks for reading this book and if you enjoyed it please tell your friends or leave a review.

Books by Bex Archer

for 3-5 year olds:
Alfie's Big Winter Sleep
Alfie and the Beach
Alfie and Flo

for 8-12 year olds:
Stone Bones

for 10-14 year olds:
Daisy Dunbar, Dragons Daughter series:
Four Dragon's Daughters
Teasel Green
Vipers Ruin
Merman's Bride
Magpie Mab